Play With Me

A Splatterpunk Dark Romance

Emily Klepp

Book Cover by Emily Klepp

Edited by: Jade Katzchen, Brittany Willaert, and Kelly Barry

1st edition 2024

Dedicated to my amazing team of editors, PAs, and my one-of-a-kind Gremlin. You all have made me not just a better author, but a better person. I am truly blessed to have you all in my life. I do not think I would be where I am today without your dedication and support. I love y'all bunches!

P.S. Thanks for the torture tips, Gremmie ;)

Contents

Play With Me VI

Your Mental Health Matters 1

1. Chapter 1 6
2. Chapter 2 19
3. Chapter 3 22
4. Chapter 4 50
5. Chapter 5 59
6. Chapter 6 68
7. Chapter 7 75
8. Chapter 8 87
9. Chapter 9 94
10. Chapter 10 100
11. Chapter 11 104
12. Chapter 12 114
13. Chapter 13 117
14. Chapter 14 122
15. Chapter 15 130
16. Chapter 16 135
17. Chapter 17 141

18. Chapter 18 154

19. Chapter 19 156

20. Chapter 20 161

21. Chapter 21 166

About the author 175

Books by this author 176

How to contact the author 177

Play With Me

Plenty of people make jokes about what they would do if a serial killer made them their target, but how many of them would beg for their lives if faced with the inevitability of death? How many would be triggered into a trauma response out of basic instinct? None of them understand true pain until all their tears have dried up and the numbness takes over. Nothing is more painful than the feeling of nothing at all. No one but the man in the shadows knows what little regard I hold for my life.

Dark humor is alright, but what if it was dark desire? What if you had the chance to have the time of your life before it was finally taken from you; someone is finally making the decision you were too indifferent to make? Would you lock your windows and doors to keep out the evil, or would you open them wide and welcome it in for tea?

The devil can't hurt me if all I've known is pain. When he finally comes out to play with me, I eagerly await my demise, until it's only our beginning.

Your Mental Health Matters

This is a splatterpunk dark romance crossover novel with <u>MANY</u> sensitive topics.

Reader's discretion is <u>HIGHLY</u> advised.
I absolutely mean it when I say this book is <u>NOT</u> for everyone.
This is your only warning!
For a full list of TW and tropes, visit edknovels.com
<u>National Domestic Violence Hotline</u>

1-800-799-7233

<u>National Sexual Assault Hotline</u>

1-800-656-4673

<u>Suicide and Crisis Lifeline</u>

988

Help IS available.

THE FOLLOWING PAGES CONTAIN A STORY THAT IS NOT FOR THE FAINT OF HEART...

STILL HERE?

Do you want to play with me?

LET THE FUN BEGIN...

Chapter One

Lila

THE POUNDING BASS REVERBERATES through the air in a downtown New York club. The scent of alcohol and the musk of sweat clings to the dance floor as bodies sway and rock. Each dancer is lost in the music. The sharp tang of cheap grocery store perfume occasionally cuts through the haze. I don't mind. To me, this smells like freedom and happiness.

They always say that the rich kids party the hardest, but that's far from the truth. This club is the cheapest in the city and I have spent less here than I would have anywhere else on one drink.

Jeff Anderson, my boyfriend of eight years, and my lifelong best friend, Jessika Patton, hate that I drag them here. They always say they hate mingling with the poor, but I think they just hate fun. Their idea of a good time is going to the fucking country club to play poker like a bunch of middle-aged Karens. I'm sure they were itching to get out of here, too.

We all live together in a two-bedroom apartment with just one bathroom. At first, they would constantly argue. Until they found plenty of things to bond over, like when I piss them off. They hate that I can be high-strung. They are always telling me I need to grow up and stop acting like a little girl, but my bills are paid, and I don't spend an excessive amount of money like they do. I have a great job and I am financially stable. I never have to touch my trust because my job provides just fine for me. At least now they can be in the same space without fighting.

When I get up to the bar and look around and still can't find them, I step outside to call Jeff. "Hello?" he says breathlessly, the sounds of some B-horror movie playing in the background.

"Hey, where did y'all go? I've been looking everywhere for you," I say.

"We went home, Lila," he grunts. I can hear what sounds like mumbled whispers in the background.

"Why do you sound like that?" I ask. "Why the fuck would you ditch me in the middle of New York City at night?"

"We told you we were leaving. We never even wanted to go there to begin with," he groans, but tries to cover it up with a cough.

Was that a moan I heard? You have got to be fucking kidding me.

"What are y'all doing? Do you mind if I hang out for a while longer?" I say as I walk toward our apartment.

"Just watching a movie," he says. "How long will you be?"

"Oh, I'll be a while," I lie. He has his dick down her throat. I know that sound he just made. I recognize those slurping sounds. I should have fucking known better than to move that skank in with us.

Yes, she's a skank. She always has been. She will let anyone with a dick fuck her. She has fucked everyone from my dad to her cousin. It's like a fucking disease and the main symptom is she can't get her goddamn legs out of the air. And Jeff? Well, let's just say he would let a raccoon chew on his dick if he thought it might get him off.

This isn't the first time he's cheated on me. If I catch him with his dick in my friend, I'm going to lose my goddamn mind. I keep wanting to blame myself, but I'm not the one who cheated. They left without telling me so they could go home and fuck around. How long has this been going on? Did they only agree to come out tonight so they could ditch me to hook up? Fuck, I'm such an idiot.

"Okay, well I'm going to grab another shot. I'll text you when I'm walking back," I say.

"Mhmm," he moans. "Yeah... Oh God... Yes... Uh... see ya later." Jeff abruptly hangs up. I am seething as I stomp my way down the sidewalk. I am wearing a short strapless dress. It shows off my tits perfectly and it hardly holds my rounded ass. My fishnets and five-inch heels pair perfectly with the rest of the outfit. I look sexy as fuck, and I feel good about myself for a change. My long, platinum blonde hair falls in beautiful curls down my back. The contrast between my bright hair and sun-kissed skin is like a work of art. It sways in the wind as I walk down the sidewalk on this beautiful early summer night.

My heels click against the concrete. I see some men standing alone a block ahead, so I cross to the other side. Maybe it's rude of me to assume they have nefarious intentions, but I don't feel like finding out. It's one in the morning and I am alone in the city. I fucking hate Jeff for ditching me. I bet he wouldn't leave Jessika to walk fifteen blocks home alone at night.

About three blocks up, I cross back over to continue my walk. The more time that passes, the more on edge I become. I think it's all in my head, until I hear it. I'm not going to turn around because that will only slow me down, but I can hear a set of footsteps in sync with him close by. They get closer and closer to me until they are no longer hiding themselves.

"Hey, sexy," he says as he quickly bands his arm around my waist and pulls me to a stop.

"Stop. Let go of me," I demand and try to pull away.

"How much for your ass, slut?" he asks. "Ten?"

"Fuck you," I spit.

"I said," he growls as he grabs me by the throat and slams me against the brick building. "How much for your ass?"

"I'm not for sale. Please let me go," I whimper. "My boyfriend is expecting me home."

"Oh, everything is for sale," he laughs. "Take her inside."

I don't understand what he means until a hand slaps over my mouth. I try to scream as I am dragged into a seemingly abandoned building. I thrash, trying to free myself from his tight hold on me. He is so much stronger than I am, but I don't give up.

He stops and shoves me to the ground and suddenly I am surrounded by men. There are at least six of them. No, eight. They look like a gang the way they are dressed. "Stop. Please stop. Please let me go," I beg from the dirt covered floor.

"Stop. Please stop. Please let me go," he mocks me in a high-pitched baby voice as he leans down and rips the front of my dress, letting my breasts spill out. I quickly cross my arms over my chest as I start to cry. "Strip her. Leave the heels on," he says.

The men converge on me, and hands are coming from everywhere as fabric is ripped from my body. "Stop. Please stop. Let me go. I won't tell anyone. Just let me go," I beg over and over, my voice cracking as tears stream down my cheeks.

My fishnets are used to tie my wrists together. One man forces me to my knees and holds my wrists behind my head. I am sobbing so hard that I can barely breathe.

The first man comes back over while another man tosses a disgusting brown mattress on the floor in front of me. "What's your name?" he asks.

"Lila," I say through my sobs.

"Good. We have the right whore. Here's the thing Lila, my boys here are hungry and I owe them some pussy," he says as he roughly grabs my chin so I can't look away. "If you want to make this as painless as possible, I suggest you be a good girl and let them fuck your tight little body, got it?"

"Please don't," I whimper. "Please."

"Beg, Lila. Scream as loud as you want, but if you fight us once, I'll put a bullet in your head while we fuck your bloody corpse," he says before his grin grows devious. "But first, I'm going to take me a little something before they fill you with come."

He gives me no time to process his words before he grabs me by the hair and shoves me face first into the rancid mattress. He then drags me up to my knees. My body is vibrating from how hysterical I've become. I can feel as he spreads my ass cheeks and flinch as his spit dribbles between my cheeks and settles. Time slows as he swirls his spit around my asshole before he rams his dick deep inside of me. I scream so loud that my voice cracks, but I don't move unless he moves me.

"Fuck. Bleed for me bitch. This is *my* tight little virgin ass," he grunts as he forces his way into my asshole. I can feel my skin ripping as it stretches to fit him.

"Please stop. It hurts. Please," I beg. "Stop. Please stop it. I'll do anything. Please stop."

The more I beg, the harder he pounds into my now bleeding ass. I can smell metallic tang of blood in the air, and I know it's coming from me. His fingers dig deep into my hips. Eventually, I've screamed so much that my voice is raspy, but he keeps going. Waves of sharp pain ripple through my abdomen as he groans loudly.

"Take my come, whore," he growls as he pushes deeper than my body wants and drains himself inside me.

"Damn, the bitch knows how to take a cock," a man laughs.

"Have at her, boys," he says. "Just don't kill her too quickly."

I am flipped onto my back. My body lies limp as a greasy looking man shoves his way between my legs, pushing them apart as he kneels between them. I've given up on begging for mercy at this point, but I can't stop the tears from falling. The greasy man pulls his dick out and forces me to wrap my hand around him, he keeps a firm grip on me as he fucks my hand, getting himself ready to assault me.

"You're such a pretty little bitch," he says with an evil smirk. Despite his smile, he rears back and slaps me across the face, making me cry out in pain. He does it again and again until I stop making noise when he hits me. That's what he needed. He needed me to submit to the pain.

He waves someone else over as he lowers himself. "Touch me with your teeth and I'll shove them down your throat," another man says as he hits me in the face with his dick. "Swallow my cock, whore." He forces my mouth open then straddles my face to thrust down my throat. The greasy man pulls my legs up and has the man currently in my throat hold them up for him. This elevates my hips to give him better access for when he starts to aggressively dry fuck me.

Both men chip away at my soul; stealing pieces of my will to live. Each thrust the greasy man makes into me makes a squelching noise as my blood coats his dick. The man in my throat is furiously pumping into me until he finally groans and fills my mouth with his thick come.

"Swallow, bitch. Drink my come," he says as he covers my mouth and pinches my nose closed. Eventually I give in and swallow, only to violently retch at the salty taste. As I gag and dry heave, the greasy man moans and pushes deep to come.

They move away from me, but three men come over and I am pulled into someone's lap. There is no lead in or warm up before they go from nothing to all three of them forcing themselves into me and continuing the trend of stealing from my body. They laugh and mock my whimpers as they rape me. My body hurts so badly, but my soul hurts worse.

Two more men come up and I am pulled on top of one as another is behind me. When they both start to rape me, the pain is so intense, even with the lubrication from the mixture of blood and come, that I scream with a raspy and worn-out voice. It feels like I am being ripped apart with how they are both aggressively thrusting into me. The man in my ass grabs me by the hair and yanks my head back.

“Let’s both fuck this tight ass,” the man behind me says.

“Fuck, that’s going to be so damn tight, he laughs as he pulls out of my vagina. I am then repositioned so that I am facing the man who was behind me. He drapes my legs over his arms while he and the other man keep a tight hold on my waist and hips. They have me angle back so they can effectively push into my ass at the same time.

“Fuuuck,” they both groan in unison as they shove their way into my ass. The pain nearly causes me to black out when they start thrusting viciously into my body. I just want this to end already but they simultaneously decide to move to my vagina. The pain is just as intense, and I suddenly scream when one of then pinches and rolls my clit in their fingers.

“Come for us, filthy whore,” one of them growls.

“Stop,” I whimper, my voice is weak and hoarse. “Please… I don’t…”

“Oh… but you will,” the man in front of me snickers. They start moving faster, pushing deeper, as a third appears and starts to rub my clit. The forced waves of a weak orgasm start to ripple through my abdomen, feeling like sharp needles. My body tenses, which only makes the men groan and slam into me harder before coming.

By the time all the men have used my body, I can’t move or speak. I stay laying on my side, staring at a clump of dirt on the ground. I can hear them mumbling something, but I can’t make it out. I just wish they would end my agony and shoot me. Hell, I don’t care how they do it, as long as I’m dead when they’re done.

This morning, I was so happy and filled with life. I was excited to go out and to get through the weekend and return to work on Monday. Now… now I am done existing. It was a good twenty-two year run, but I’m done now. Why do I want to exist in a world where people do these things to others?

I never did anything to deserve this. I never hurt anyone. I help old people with their groceries, and I pay my taxes. I don't judge people for how they choose to live their life or who they love, but karma decided that I had a lesson to learn. Maybe it was God. They say that God does everything for a reason. What reason led to me being gang raped by eight men?

I have mostly disassociated but I know they are still close by. After a while, I get dragged up to my knees. The first man pulls his dick out again as he fists my hair to yank my head back. "Open up, cum-dumpster," he says with a vile grin. I don't react fast enough for him, so he slaps me across the face. "Come on, now... open that pretty little mouth before I break your teeth."

Tears stream down my cheeks, but I do as I'm told. When I open my mouth, he grabs the sides of my face and thrusts himself down my throat. I violently gag when he pushes in, and he starts hitting the same spot repeatedly. I can feel the bile rising in my throat, so I try to pull away. He tightens his grip on my head and continues his assault. I try to keep it down, but he is relentless and clearly determined to make me throw up.

"That's it, bitch." He laughs when my body rejects everything and I vomit. It has nowhere to go, and my body keeps turning inside out, trying to get rid of the intrusion. It comes out of my nose and the sides of my mouth. The men laugh heartily as I continue to puke uncontrollably. When he finally pulls away, I am covered in my own vomit. I fall to my hands and throw up again, my body desperate to feel better.

A sudden piercing blow to my head makes the world go fuzzy as I get shoved further onto the disgusting mattress. I am surrounded by all the men; I can hear the sickening sounds of them jerking off. One of the men reaches between my legs to wipe blood and come mixture from me to lubricate himself. One after another, they all come on my face and chest as I lie unmoving. I am so weak and numb that I hardly notice that a few of them begin to piss on me until one of them intentionally sprays it in my mouth. I inadvertently gasp when he does this and instantly start heaving again until I throw up. I can hardly move, the only thing I can manage is to turn my head, so I don't breathe it in.

A rancid smell of raw shit fills the air as I feel someone smear something on my chest. "Dog shit for the bitch," a man laughs.

"Go wash your hands, nasty ass," another man laughs.

"It was so nice to finally meet you, Lila," the first man says as he squats down to look at me. "Tell Jeff we said hello... if you make it that long."

I am confused by his words, but I don't get a chance to question anything before another hit makes the world go dark.

I feel a heavy weight on my body as my brain is trying to drag me to consciousness. I am moving... no... rocking. Someone is on top of me... I try to move my hands, but they are pinned under me. I force my eyes open to see a man on me. He has his eyes closed as he fucks my limp body. His arms are hooked behind my knees as he pumps into me. He is dirty, probably homeless. He isn't being violent, and I appreciate that, oddly enough.

I unintentionally groan as disgusting pleasure sneaks up on me and his eyes snap open. "Oh, such pretty eyes, girl... you like how this cock makes you feel... mmm, you're gripping me so tight."

He pushes my knees to my chest and starts to fuck me harder. At this point, I don't give a fuck. At least he's not hurting me. Somehow, I'd rather get raped by someone who wants to force me to come rather than someone who wants to piss in my mouth and spread dog shit on my chest.

The homeless man finds a spot that makes me moan and keeps hitting it over and over until eventually I come. He keeps pounding me through my orgasm and straight into another until he finally pulls out and jerks himself until he comes on my belly. He brings my legs down and grabs something from his bag. I close my eyes and just try and pretend it's a gun. Maybe he's going to do me and the world a favor by blowing my brains out.

Unfortunately, it's hygiene. He cleans my limp body while I lay on the mattress. When he gets done, he rolls me to my side and unties my wrists. "I ain't going down for what those men did but… I'll send someone down here to get you," he says. He pats my leg gently before laying a dirty blanket across my body and walking out with his bag.

My head is throbbing and my body aches. I just want to take a shower and jump off something tall. None of this would have happened if they hadn't ditched me. I can see a light beam shine onto the dirty floor from outside. How long was I out? Do they even care that I never came home?

"Oh, sweetie," I hear a kind feminine voice say. "Let's get you some help. Come on."

The woman scoops me up with the blanket wrapped around my body. She grabs my purse and lays it on my abdomen before walking me out of the building. For some reason, I feel safe with her.

"My name is Mildred. What's yours?" she asks as she carries me.

"Lila," I whisper.

"What happened?"

"My boyfriend and best friend ditched me, and I had to walk home alone," I say with a hoarse voice. I don't know why I am telling her this. "They were following me."

"They? How many?" she asks.

"Eight."

"My goodness," she sighs. "Ah here's a cop. Excuse me, officer?" she calls out to get his attention.

"Is she okay?" the man asks. Checking on me. "She on anything?"

"No. I found her in the old flower shop up the road. She said eight men... well... she's been hurt. She's got blood all over her thighs," Mildred says.

The man gets on his radio and calls for help before having Mildred sit me on steps. "What's your name?"

"Lila Monroe," I say. "I think I have my phone. Can I call my boyfriend?"

"Yes. Have him meet you at the hospital. When was this?" he asks.

"I... I was walking home around one and... after all of them got done... The first guys hit me. I didn't wake up until just a little bit ago when... right before Mildred found me. She untied my arms." I'm hoping Mildred doesn't call out my lie in front of the cop. The homeless man did rape me... But he also untied me. He could have left me there to die, but he didn't. That's got to count for something.

I get my phone out of my bag and see that I have over a hundred missed calls between Jeff and Jessika. I dial Jeff first since he called me last.

"Lila. Where the fuck are you?" Jeff asks.

"Jeff," I say as I suddenly start to cry.

"Lila... what's wrong? Where are you?" he asks.

"I... you'll have to meet me at the hospital. I'm... I'm with a cop... I..."

"Lila... what happened?" he asks. "We are coming. What happened? Where were you?"

"I was trying to walk home... I heard what you two were doing and... I was walking home to catch you... they were following me. I screamed and begged but... I was just trying to go home... and Jeff?"

"Fuck... I'm so sorry honey. I'm so fucking sorry," he says.

"They told me to tell you hi... if I made it that long," I tell him when the cop walks away to greet the ambulance. "I don't know what the fuck you just got me into but fix it. *Now.*" The sudden rush of anger in my voice surprises me.

"Fuck... shit, okay. I'll fix it. I'm sorry. I didn't think..."

"Yeah," I snap. "You didn't fucking think. You two fucking left me. This fucking happened because you cared more about getting your dick sucked by my best friend."

"I'm sorry, Lila. I swear to God, I'll make it up to you," he says softly.

"You wanna make it up to me? You find the eight men who brutally raped me and left me for dead. You go back in time and walk home with me. You go back and not get involved with scum like that. Think you can do that?" I ask calmly.

"Ready?" the officer asks me.

"Meet me at the fucking hospital," I say before ending the call. "Sorry."

"No, ma'am. You don't apologize," Mildred says. "You just find new people to associate with. Friends don't let friends walk home alone. Don't even get me started on your moron boyfriend." I can't help but laugh at her disdain for Jeff.

Mildred stands and helps me up. The cop helps support me so I can keep the blanket around me. Who knows where the fuck my shoes went. "Do you have a phone, Mildred?"

"I do," she smiles.

"Think I could call you some time?" I ask. I don't know why, but I just love her aura. It has a soft pink glow and it's comforting.

"Yes, baby. You can call me anytime you'd like," she says. "Want me to come with you?"

"Uh... just until they get there... if that's okay?"

"Yeah," she smiles. I hand her my phone so she can add her number in, then calls herself so she has my number too.

"Okay," I smile briefly. The paramedic takes over and helps me into the back of the ambulance. Once I get situated, the cop tells me that he will have someone come to take my statement.

Chapter Two

Nash

I DRAG THE BLADE across his trachea, savoring the gurgles he makes as his throat floods with blood. I can't help but grin when his eyes go wide and the panic shows on his face as blood spurts out in sync with his heartbeat. The deep crimson liquid coats the front of my navy blue coveralls. A ribbon of blood splatters across my face shield which makes me laugh. And to think I almost forgot to bring it with me.

This fucker, I can't remember his name now, but he decided it was a good idea to beat his wife bloody. He sat in front of that judge today and lied. Lied about the abuse, the violence, the drinking. Just like Dad did with us... look where that got me.

The moment I saw him, his aura was pitch black. His soul was ruined by the darkness. I knew right then that he had to die. Your aura is either dark or light. You can't be benevolent but also be like a malevolent demon. You are either evil or you are not. If I see the darkness in your soul, I will make it my life mission to watch the light leave your eyes as your blood drains from your body.

The first time I killed someone, I rode that high for weeks. I killed my drunk, abusive father and burned his body in the crematorium owned by my adoptive father. Now that Jimmy is gone, the funeral home and crematorium belong to me.

Do you know how fucking convenient it is to kill as many people as I do and be able to torch the fucking evidence? This makes everything so much easier because I can just drive a hearse with a body in it and no one will think differently of it.

The funeral home isn't my day job though. I wish I could burn dead bodies all day. I run a cyber security company during the week. This job makes it easier to find targets because I can track someone digitally without leaving a trace of myself behind. No one would ever know that someone was there. That's how I found this prick. He was on some dating website looking for a fuck.

I get the freshly sharpened cleaver out and start working on his arms first. The first strike is always the most satisfying. I've had so much practice at this, his arm is nearly severed at the shoulder. The marbling of tender flesh from such precision is a beautiful sight of red and white. I have a few more chops before I move to wrap that arm in paper. I have found that the easiest way to get rid of the body is to just dismember them and add their parts in with bodies that are already going in to be cremated. This way, I'm not having to fire it up without anything on the schedule.

Through trial and error, I think I have found a foolproof way to rid the world of these dark souls. For crimes involving children or sexual assault, I like to chop their dick and balls off with my cleaver while they are alive. It's my way of getting their victims and survivors justice.

I wheel the bodies over to their respective ovens and add in the parts to the boxes before putting everything in to burn.

The next order of business is to clean up. I bleach everything and hose it down thoroughly before taking my overalls and face shield off and place it in the last box for a pet cremation.

I step outside to enjoy the early summer air as I lean against the brick wall. An ear-piercing scream from off in the distance makes me stand up straight and look around. A lot of weird shit happens in this city at one in the morning, but that... she sounded like she was in pain.

Fuck. Why does that make me hard? I would drop everything and go find that woman and save her from whatever hell she is enduring right now, but I cannot leave these bodies unattended with extra parts. I know I'll find who is making her scream like that… I'll make them pay for what they are doing to her.

The more she screams, the harder I get. Fuck, I wish I was the one making her scream. I shouldn't do this, but there is no harm done if I'm alone, right?

I pull out my cock and shame myself as I start fucking my hand. I imagine the voice closer and under me, but she's not in pain… no, she loves the way I destroy her. She loves the way I break her to pieces before putting her back together. Each time I stroke across the barbells in my cock, my body jerks. I pump faster, desperate to come for her. I want to come for her, my mystery woman whose screams are echoing in my mind. I don't know who she is or how someone I don't know has this effect on me, but I will find her and learn how to break my little butterfly.

Chapter Three

Lila

Between everyone trying to convince me to get a rape kit and the police taking my statement, it took an additional twelve hours after being found before the hospital would release me.

I have a nice list of injuries. I have a concussion, rectal tearing, a bruised cervix, tearing of the perineum, and ligature marks on my wrists from being bound so tightly. Jeff and Jessika have been trying to wait on me hand and foot, but I just need them to shut the fuck up for five goddamn seconds.

They are trying to make up for what they did and what they caused. I am blunt about how much blame they have, and I won't let them forget it either. They haven't openly admitted to fucking around, but they swore to me it was done, whatever "it" is.

I decided against the rape kit because I know that it doesn't matter. I let them do an exam as far as determining "yes, she was raped". I didn't want to be poked and prodded all over again. I just wanted to go home and shower. Wash the dirt, blood, come, piss, and dog shit off my body. The homeless man who I woke up to fucking me cleaned me up quite a bit. I'd be lying if I said he wasn't partially the reason I didn't get the swabs.

Yes, he raped me just like the others did, but he didn't leave me there to die. He didn't cause me pain. He was just a fucking creep. Maybe I made the wrong decision, but I'm doing what I can do to not kill myself right now. Everything I look at; I contemplate how I could use it to end my life. Toaster in the bath. Swallow a bottle of pills. Use the kitchen knives to slice deep into my arms and bleed out on the floor. Or I could get into my car and drive full speed into a tree. I wouldn't do a light pole because I would cause people to lose power. What if someone was on life support and I kill them? I would say that I wouldn't be able to live with myself, but I guess it wouldn't matter if I'm dead. I just don't want to cause anyone pain. Well... anyone innocent at least.

I strip off the clothes that the hospital gave me and step into the scalding hot shower. The steam takes over and I close my eyes, letting the sting of the water lull my brain. But it doesn't stop the flashes of memories from sneaking in. I start scrubbing my body, trying to cleanse myself. I don't think I'll ever feel clean again.

They did all the tests, and they all show negative for anything sexually transmitted, but I still feel unclean. No matter how much I scrub my body raw, it won't help me forget the hands that have been on me. *I hate this so fucking badly.* I just want to disappear. *I'm sick of existing.*

How am I supposed to look at the world and see anything but pain now? Every person I look at... what depraved shit would they do if given the chance? Would they be the one to hold me down and fuck my ass bloody, or would they wait until I'm unconscious to take what they want? Would they make me scream from pain or from an orgasm I never wanted? Or are they a victim? And I know... I survived it. I'm a survivor, but I wish I hadn't. I want nothing more than to swallow a bottle of pills or find a straight razor and cut until I'm too weak to lift my arms. I want my death to be painful. I want to feel every last twinge as the life drains from my body. I want my screams to be heard for blocks and blocks, exciting the minds of the sick and twisted.

I feel like I don't even know the woman I used to be. I am no longer that bright and bubbly girl who would practically bounce into the room. My voice lacks its usual warmth and happiness. Before, it didn't matter what I said because you could always tell I was happy. Now... I don't even think I know what that word means. I overheard Jeff tell Jessika that my dreary mood was dramatic, and I should be thankful I'm alive.

Should I be thankful that I'm alive? Maybe some people can fall to their knees and thank God that they lived through the situation but right now I'm cursing him for not taking me out. Why the fuck would you put someone through that just to make them live with it every day? That should've been the end of my life. No one should've found me; I should've died in that abandoned building. Maybe the enemy here is the man who freed me. Maybe it's Mildred for getting me help. She was so sweet though. She didn't coddle me or treat me like I was fragile. She was respectful. Doctors and nurses were respectful also as they explained everything before they did it.

When the water starts to turn cold, I rinse the soap from my body before shutting the water off and wrapping in a towel. Once I dry off, I dress in shorts and a big T-Shirt before going to lie in bed. I curl up on my side on the edge of the bed with the blanket pulled up to cocoon me. I hear someone walk in, but I ignore them. When they turn the light on, I bury my face in the comforter.

"Hey. Are you hungry?" Jeff asks softly.

"No," I say with a small voice.

"Lila, you need to eat," he says. He gently squeezes my shoulder, and it feels as though someone has stabbed me. I recoil and sink into the bed further to get away from his touch. "Whatever. Starve then."

Jeff leaves the room with a huff before slamming the door behind him. I feel like this should be the moment that I start crying again, but I just don't have it in me anymore. I should yell and scream at him for not caring. I told him and Jessika the real story. I told them all the horrible things they said and did. I told them how my savior was a homeless man who just wanted to take from me. How could he be so callous when this is his fault? Does he care that nine men were inside of his girlfriend? Does he care that I prayed to God for me to die? Doesn't he know that part of me was glad I wouldn't have to come home to him anymore? Would he and Jessika just go on as if I never existed? I bet they enjoyed their time together while I was missing.

I hear the door again and I roll my eyes. "What, Jessika?" I ask.

"You really should eat, Lila." she says softly.

"The thought of eating makes me want to throw up. If I throw up, I will legitimately throw myself off this building after what they did to me," I say. "I understand you two are just trying to help, but I just need to be left alone. Neither of you are required to pretend you're happy I'm home.

"What? Lila..."

"Did you fuck him?" I ask, rolling to look at her. "Did you fuck Jeff after you sucked him off while he was on the phone with me?"

"Yes," she says quietly.

"While you two were here having sex, I was being *violently* raped. While you two felt so proud that you successfully ditched me, a man was fucking me while I screamed and begged for him to stop. One after another after another fucked me while I screamed in pain until my voice was gone and my throat was raw. Men who came on me, in me, and degraded me in ways no one deserves. For what? Why? Why did they tell me to tell Jeff 'Hi'?" I say, almost screaming at her. "Now I'm back and you have the fucking audacity to pretend that you give a fuck about me when you two are just as guilty as the men who held me down."

"That's not fair," Jessika says through tears. "We didn't know you would get hurt."

"It's New York, Jessika," I scream. "What the fuck do you mean you didn't know? There has always been gang activity around here. Literally everyone has told us to never walk around at night alone but you two had no problem leaving me there and not even telling me that you left. Don't talk to me about what's fair and what's not. It's not fair that I got raped for something that Jeff did. It's not fair that while my boyfriend of eight goddamn years was getting his dick wet with my best friend, I was hoping they would kill me. It's not fair that I have to sit here and think about everything that they did and not be able to make it go away and not have the guts to kill myself. No matter how many times I boil myself in that shower or try to peel my skin off scrubbing, it won't go away. The feeling of them hurting me while you two fucked will never go away. Unless you

can make all those memories go away... unless you can go back in time and not abandon me... get the fuck out of my room and leave me the hell alone!"

She sniffs back tears before walking out of the room. Maybe I shouldn't have been such a cunt to her. Does she really deserve that much hostility from me? I want to think that maybe I am being dramatic, and I should just get the fuck over it, but I don't know how to do that.

I lay here, staring at the wall for hours before Jeff comes in for bed. I stay still and keep my breathing even, pretending to be asleep so he will leave me alone. I don't want to talk to him or get scolded for making Jessika cry. I wonder how he comforted her. Did he just cover her mouth and fuck her over the arm of the couch to make the tears go away? He did that to me once. I bet he held her close and told her it would be okay. "One day she will kill herself and we will be rid of her," I imagine him saying.

My thoughts are cut off when he wraps his arms around my waist and kisses my shoulder. "I'm so sorry," he whispers. "They weren't supposed to touch you and I can't fix it."

"Was it gambling debt again?" I ask.

"Lila..." he starts.

"Don't bullshit me, Jeff. Was it?"

"Yes. About a half million. I couldn't pay them back on time and I thought they'd come after me... Then he texted me saying we were even now," he says.

"You knew?" I roll to my back and ask. "You knew I was out there somewhere hurt, and you didn't do anything?"

"I thought he killed you," he says.

"You didn't even try to find me," I say as I shove his hand off me.

"Lila, please," he pleads.

"Why are you fighting for me like you want me?" I ask.

"We've been together for eight years, Lila," he says.

"You fucked my best friend, Jeff," I say. "You think I want to be with you after you were fucking my best friend while I was gang raped by men that you owed money to? Do you know what it's like to be in so much pain that you wanna die? Do you know what it's like to be so fucking numb that you wish that somebody would take you out? I hate that fucking man for saving me. He should have just let me lay there and die. Instead, I'm stuck having this goddamn conversation with you."

"Can I fix this? Is it possible?" he asks with a sigh.

"No, Jeff. You can't fix this," I say.

"Then what do you want from me? Do you want to just coexist as roommates? Do you want her and I to leave?" he asks.

"I want you to get the fuck out of this bedroom and let me sleep. When I have more energy, I'm going somewhere else. You two can have the apartment," I say.

"You need to heal, Lila," he says.

"Worry about yourself," I say. "You're best at that. Caring boyfriend doesn't look good on you anymore."

"I want to fix this, Lila," he says.

"Can you sit here and promise me that you will never touch her again? That you will be able to work with me on every single trigger that I will have and not get mad when I can't have sex with you? Can you live with the possibility that it could take months before I can be intimate with you and not get triggered?" I ask. His silence speaks so loudly. "That's what I thought... so, just go sleep with Jessika. Live your life and just forget about me. I absolve you from any guilt that you have so long as you just leave me the fuck alone."

"Okay," he says. "When will you go?"

"I don't know," I say honestly. "I want to sleep."

"I'll go," he says. Jeff gets up and comes around to kneel beside me. He gently cups my face and is lost in thought. "It was never supposed to be this way, Lila. I'm sorry I failed you."

"Goodbye, Jeff," I say flatly. He sighs and leans down to kiss my forehead before leaving the room. When the door clicks shut, I close my eyes.

I open my eyes to the sound of moans, and I sigh. It's like they are rubbing it in. They win because they weren't the one to get unwillingly fucked bloody.

I get out of bed and go down the hall to the living room to find Jeff balls deep in Jessika as she is bent over the couch. They both jump up and move away from one another. "Don't let me interrupt," I say. "Just getting some headache medicine before I pack."

I continue walking through the kitchen. There's not really anything in here that I want to keep, so they can have it all. I do take all of the bottles of medicine that I have in here just in case I feel like killing myself.

"You don't have to go," Jeff says from behind me.

"Oh? So, I can be so lucky as to hear you doing that? How wonderful would that be to hear my ex-boyfriend and my ex-best friend fucking while I grieve the loss of myself. Get fucking real, Jeff. I'll be out in a few hours. Call and take your name off my bank account. Now."

"Okay," he says simply.

"Go finish fucking your girlfriend. It's not nice to leave her without an orgasm," I say as I take a sip of water to wash the headache medicine down.

"Lila... Jessika is pregnant," he says.

"Congratulations," I say as I push past him to go to the bedroom. I shut and lock the door so they will leave me alone. I find my earbuds and put them in before blaring music. My mind is silent this way. I grab some bags down and start packing my clothes. I only take the basic stuff because I don't plan on continuing to work. I have the trust but even then, I just don't give a fuck. I plan on staying in my car anyway. I need to figure out where I can park without getting towed.

I grab my journals and pens so I can write. I don't know what I'll write about, but I want to have that option. I take all my jewelry and anything I can get money for. I don't need it anymore so I'm just going to turn it into cash. I'm taking two bags when I can easily fill my car completely with my crap. I just don't see the use in everything anymore. I decide to bring my make-up and a few dresses with matching heels. Maybe it's stupid, but I kind of want to go out again. If I'm going to get raped every time I try to have fun, I might as well get shitfaced drunk while I'm at it. Maybe it won't hurt as bad when they pound into me if I'm drunk.

I take my bags to sit by the front door before finding other essentials like hygiene items, chargers, and a protein bar so I don't fall over. I'll have to get some food that can sit in my car and not rot.

"You really don't have to do this," Jessika says. "We can leave."

"How sweet of you," I say with a fake smile. "How long have you two been fucking?"

"Two years as of yesterday," Jeff says.

"Aw. Happy anniversary. Consider this my present to you," I say before I go to the kitchen and grab the boxes of protein bars that we have stored. Jessika and I both eat these as meal replacements, but now I think it's the only thing I can stomach. I know I want to die being in pain, but I don't think starving to death is the pain that I'm talking about. I have to eat something.

"The power is in my name, but I don't care if you leave it. Not my problem if you don't pay it and it gets shut off," I say. "Is your name off my account?"

"Yes," Jeff says.

"Did you take anything?" I ask.

"What? No. That's your money," he says.

"You should have. Maybe if you had a little bit set aside the next time you owe somebody money you can just pay them rather than getting someone gang raped. Wouldn't that suck if that happened to both of your girlfriends? Trust me when I say they would have fun with her. They had the time of their lives with me."

"Why are you so fucking morbid all of a sudden?" he says with a callous tone.

"Stop it," Jessika scolds him. "Lila... I know you hate me, and I deserve it... but please know I'm here if you need to talk. Don't make me have to go to your funeral because you couldn't ask for help."

"I don't want you at my funeral so don't worry about that," I say. "And I know I could get help, but I don't want it. What I want to do is to die in peace. You two are not what I consider peace anymore."

"Lila, you don't mean that," she says tearfully. "Please..."

"Jessika... just stop," I say. "I'm leaving my work laptop here. I'll tell Daniel where he can pick it up."

"Lila, you're scaring me," Jeff says. "We can help..."

"I think you have done quite enough damage, Jeff," I say with a grave tone. "Leave me alone. Both of you."

I grab my bags and take them to my car. I'm well aware of the pain in my body and my head, but I just need to get out of here. I can rest later. I might pay for a hotel for a few weeks so I can rest somewhere comfortably. I have nearly four million in a bank account right now, so I could survive off this. Maybe one day I will have the will to live, and I can replenish everything. Right now, I'm just going to make sure I have the bare minimum so I can be safe but alone."

I have to be careful where I park my car because it's almost brand new. Someone will steal this thing in a heartbeat if I park in the wrong spot. Then I really will be homeless.

I get into my car. Jeff grabs me and hugs me tightly. I tense up but let him do it. "Please choose to live," he whispers.

"If not, you know how to get a hold of my parents," I say flatly and I pull away from him. "I hope you two have the life that you deserve."

Before either of them can make some bullshit excuse to keep talking to me, I get into my car and lock the doors. I look around and I have plenty of room in here. My seats fold down so I can sleep and then in the back there's room for storing things. I'll have to go to the dollar store and buy some organizational things, so I don't go completely insane here. For now, I'm going to find a motel. I want one that's cheap, but not one that I will get raped in my sleep again or shot through the wall.

I drive around for a while until I find something. There are a few prostitutes, but they don't look like they are on drugs. I will avoid the places where people look to be strung out. These girls just look like they are trying to make a living. They smile at me when I walk from the front office to my car so I can move it in front of the room that they assigned me to. I asked to be a little further away, so he put me at the very far end of the motel on the ground floor. I told him I was going to stay here for a while, and he seemed to be content knowing that. I was just warned that I would have to get out if I brought drugs in and they found out. He did tell me that pot didn't matter, so maybe I'll take up smoking weed. Maybe that will calm me down.

Once I get everything in my room, I decide to call Mildred. The phone only rings twice before she picks up. "Lila," she says happily.

"Hey. Uh... do you have time to meet?" I ask. I don't know why I asked that, but I just need to be near her, I think.

"Yes, of course, dear. Where are you?"

"I am at a motel right now, but I can meet you in town. Do you know the coffee shop on Elm, I think it's called The Drip, or something.

"Yeah. I know where that is," she says. "I can be there in about twenty minutes. I just need to find a place to park."

"I'll walk that way. I'm only a few blocks away," I say.

"No, ma'am. I'll come pick you up," she says. "Are you at Willards Motel? It has that bar next door I think."

"Yeah. I'm on the end, furthest from the office. I'm on the ground floor," I say. "I can walk. It's not a problem."

"No, Lila. You were hurt badly. You shouldn't be walking around. It will only make it worse," she says. "Never mind the fact that you will have to pass by that place again."

"Wouldn't that suck... get dragged in for a second time," I say, laughing dryly.

"It would," she agrees. It's refreshing that she didn't scold my dark humor. "I'm right around the corner so meet me outside."

"Okay. Thank you", I say.

When we get off the phone, I change out of my jean shorts and into knit pants. They are a bit more comfortable, especially if I'm going to be moving around. I keep my giant T-shirt on but at least I have a bra on now. I slipped my feet into some simple flats and step out with my phone and wallet in hand.

A cute little sedan pulls up. I thought that she was homeless since he went and got her, but I don't think she is. She was very well put together. I don't know why I assumed that she was homeless. "Hey, sweetie," she says when I open the car door.

"Hey," I say as I ease myself into the seat.

"How are you feeling?" she asks as she pulls away from the motel.

"Very sore," I say. "Thanks for meeting me. I just didn't want to be alone I guess."

"It's not a problem," she smiles. "Shouldn't you be at home though?"

"Well... Jeff and Jessika got on my nerves, pretending like they gave a shit about me. I'm so sick and tired of existing. If I have to exist, I don't wanna have to do it near them. I told Jeff last night that I was done, that he could have Jessika and I would go away. I told him just to get out and let me sleep and when I woke up, I would pack my stuff. I woke to them fucking in the living room. They tried to pretend like they cared again so I just packed my shit and left. I did remember to get Jeff off of my bank account though."

"That's good. I mean, it's not good that you are living in a motel now, but" she says. "I have room if you want to come stay with me. Even if it's just until you heal."

"No, I have a trust fund that I have access to. There's enough for me to survive without having to work. I will pull myself out of this fog or I'll kill myself and it'll go back to my parents," I say.

"Do you want to kill yourself?" she asks.

"Honestly, yeah. I don't think I have the courage to do it though. It takes a lot of fucking guts to do something like that. I'm afraid that if I fuck it up, I'll just end up disabled and unable to help myself."

"So, if you don't want to die, what do you want?"

"I want to learn how to make it stop hurting," I say. "Every time I close my eyes, I see their faces. I think they intended for me to die in there. I wish that man had just taken what he wanted and left me there. He didn't have to help me."

"Roy? What did he do?" she asks.

"The guy that untied me? I woke up to him fucking me. When he noticed I woke, he went harder until he forced me to come, then untied me."

"Jesus Christ. He's..."

"Nuts?" I ask "Yeah. I gathered that. I didn't tell the cops about him because he didn't hurt me. Still fucked up that he thought it was okay to fuck an unconscious woman, but he didn't cause me any pain. Even though I hate him for saving me, he didn't have to do that."

"I'll handle him. He needs to be in a home anyway. I've been trying to get someone to take him before he hurts someone, but no one will take him," she says. "Maybe they'll listen to me now."

We get to a parking garage and were lucky to find a spot on the bottom level. All we have to do is walk around the corner and the coffee shop is right there. When we get sat down, I instantly feel like I'm being watched. When I look around, no one is looking at me. I think I'm just on edge because this is the first time I've been in public since the rape. It was nearly twenty-four hours after the first rape before I got to go home. Then I slept for eighteen hours.

"I should be going to work tomorrow," I say as Mildred and I sit in a corner booth. I am in the corner so I can see everyone and it's comforting this way.

"But you aren't?" she asks.

"No," I say. "I need to call my boss and quit."

"Need or want?" she asks.

"Both. I just... I'm done. I don't know if that means that maybe I will kill myself or if I just need a massive change in my life," I explain. "Friday morning, I was happy and bubbly. Nothing bad could ever happen. The world was full of sunshine and warmth... but now... now it feels like I'm in Hell. Either I accept it or find my way out."

"You can accept living in Hell without letting it consume you," she says. "This rape... it will haunt you for the rest of your life. I won't sugarcoat it when I say that you will have flashbacks years from now... but you will learn to navigate it.

You might see the world for all of its darkness now, but that light still exists. All you have to do is let it in."

"What if I'm never ready to let it in?" I ask. "What if the dark brings me comfort?"

"Baby, whatever keeps you out of the morgue is okay by me," she says. "It will take time and patience, but you will get there."

"Why are you so sure?"

"Because I think you are far stronger than you know," she says. "I went through a similar situation when I was twenty."

"Oh?" I ask.

"Mhmm. I drank a bit too much and let a bunch of frat guys take me to my home," she says. "Well... they said they would take me home. What they really did was take me back to the frat house and pass me around to fifteen people. I didn't tell anyone about it, but I ended up pregnant from the rape. One of the guys tracked me down and beat the fuck out of me until I lost the baby and ultimately my uterus."

"My God," I say. "I'm so sorry."

"It was a long time ago, but it still hurts. That pain does not consume my life though. You will get to the point where you can navigate it and still function. Your only job right now is to heal and survive. You can't let them take more from you right now, you have your life, so live it."

"Yeah," I sigh. "I think for now, I'm just going to sit in the hotel, eat junk food, and watch TV. Between college and my job, I have never had time to just sit and exist without having responsibilities. Even growing up, my parents always had me doing some bullshit. It was either etiquette class or piano lessons or some other dumb bullshit I had no interest in."

"Well, I will come visit you every day. I know I don't have to, and I know you probably don't want me to, but I'm going to," she says.

"It's like you knew what I'd say," I say with a smirk, and she laughs.

"You and I are a lot alike, dear," she says, patting my hand.

"Oddly enough, I'm okay with being around you. I think you are the only one who I seem to actually want to be around."

"Well, eventually you'll have to make some friends that are at least within twenty years of your age," she says. "But I'll be the momma that I know you need."

"I want to be angry or sad or I don't know. I want to feel something… but I'm just so numb. I don't care about anything. As long as my basic needs are met for survival, I don't care. I just left an eight-year relationship like it was nothing. I walked away from my best friend and didn't even hesitate. I'm about to make a call to quit my dream job. I spent four years in school to get this job and now… I don't care. I feel like my entire life has fallen apart… it's like the moment he put his hands on me I died. Right there on that sidewalk… I drew my last breath of freedom. Now, I'm a prisoner of my mind and I can't find the goddamn key to get out. I don't even think I want out. I just want someone to run a red light when I'm crossing the road. Maybe a drunk driver to swerve off the road and run me down…"

"Lila… you'll find someone one day who will make you feel whole again. He will fill in the gaps of your soul and give you a reason to get up every morning. Maybe this is the change that you need in your life to get where you need to go. Does it make it right that you had to be brutalized to get there? No, absolutely not. I wish the universe had different ways to teach us lessons but if I had never been attacked the way I was, I never would've learned to love myself. I met my husband and two beautiful children. I wouldn't have my grandchildren. You will look back one day and realize that while it sucked that you went through it, there is a silver lining in every bit of the trauma."

"How am I supposed to see the silver lining when I can't even see myself alive tomorrow?" I ask as a single tear falls down my cheek.

"You focus on the silver lining for today," she says. "You left your boyfriend, your best friend, your home, your job. But you're free. You clearly have the money to survive without being bound to a job, so do what you want to do. If you wanna go out and get trash drunk every night, just call me for a ride. If you wanna go fuck everything with a dick, make them wear a condom. If you want to sit in that motel and cry, I'll bring you some tissues," she says. "You have your whole life ahead of you, baby girl. But you are not required to think about the rest of your life right at this moment. You get to sit and do whatever the fuck you want and heal. So be content that you have that bank account. That is your silver lining for the day."

"I'm glad that you don't make everything sound so easy," I say.

"It's not easy. Anyone who thinks it's easy to get over something like that is a fool. You can't just wish away the pain when you have someone violate you like that. What those men did to you, was atrocious and it's going to take more than just a simple pep talk and a coffee shop to give you the will to live," she says.

"I feel like I'm always being watched," I say. She looks around at everyone before looking at me.

"Sometimes I still feel like people are watching me," she says. "Sometimes I fear that someone will come up behind me and I won't be able to react in my old age."

"I should make this call," I sigh and pull my phone out. I scroll to my boss's number and hit the green call button.

"Hello?" he answers.

"Hey, Daniel," I say. "I need to talk to you. I called because I wanted to do this over the phone, so I didn't have to come into the office and do it... but..."

"What's wrong, Lila? Are you okay?" he asks.

"No... uh... can you meet me downtown?"

"Yeah. I'm with my wife but we can meet up. Where are you?" I tell him where I am and let him know that I have someone with me. I don't know why I told him that. I guess part of me wants to be cautious, but he literally just said his wife was with him. Also, he's never given me bad vibes. I thought I would never be in this position, but here we are nine men later.

Mildred and I sit in silence, drinking our coffee. When I hear a familiar voice behind me, I flinch. "Lila," Daniel says. "Woah. Sorry. I didn't mean to scare you."

"I'm Mildred," she says, offering Daniel her hand since I suddenly can't speak or look at him. I'm so afraid of seeing the same look in his eye that I saw in those men's eyes Friday night.

"Daniel," he says. "I am her supervisor at Papillon Security Management."

"You work at Papillon?" Mildred asks me.

"Mhmm. I'm a computer engineer. I just finished up my master's a few months ago," I say. "I did six years of work and four years off for nothing."

"Can we sit?" The woman with him asks, and I nod. "I'm Allison, Daniel's wife."

"What's going on?" Daniel asks.

"I... I quit," I say, unable to look up. "I just need... I don't actually know what I need. I just can't do it. My laptop is at home. Well, I guess it's not my home. The laptop is at my old apartment with Jeff and Jessika."

"Were they..."

"Fucking? Yeah. She's pregnant," I say. "I found out Friday night... and I uh... was trying to go home to catch them after they ditched me downtown..." I stop abruptly and look at Mildred. I can't say the words, but I want him to know that it's not his fault. He's a great guy and a wonderful boss.

"Want me to explain everything?" she asks, taking my hand in hers. I nod tearfully and keep staring into my coffee cup.

"Friday night she was attacked and raped by eight men. They left her for dead, tied up in an abandoned building. I found her the next afternoon. She was at the hospital for a while but finally got to go home. She then decided she didn't want to be around Jeff and Jessika. She packed up her things and is now staying in a motel for a while to clear her head and find a path to take next."

"Oh, Lila," he says softly, wiping tears from his face.

"I just can't bring myself to go into that office every day. I don't want to be here... I just. I'm tired of living but I'm trying to find a balance that doesn't end with me killing myself. The things that they did... it was more than just degrading. I don't know if I will ever look at the world in a positive light again and I don't want to bring that into the office. It's a workplace not a therapy office and I don't think I can separate my trauma from my work right now," I say, crying. "I love my job. I don't wanna do this, but I don't have a choice if I want to survive."

"Come here," he says. When he moves his chair slightly closer to me and puts his arms out, I instinctively let him hug me. When he does, I fall apart. "You don't have to quit, Lila. Your job will be here when you're ready."

"The world can't stop for me, Daniel," I sniff as I pull back to wipe my face.

"I know you haven't been there long but believe me when I say that the owner would be more than happy to give you all the time that you need to heal. I will go get your laptop and bring it to you. If you want to work, I will email you some stuff and you can work remotely. If you want to take some time off, I will keep your job for you."

"Daniel, I don't know how long it will take," I say. "I don't even know if I can survive."

"Make this one less thing you have to worry about. It's one less thing that you're losing," he says. "They don't take everything from you, you hear me? You have your life, you have your job, and you have a roof over your head. I will talk to Mr. Sutton and knowing him, he's going to continue to pay you."

"I don't deserve to get paid if I'm not working, Daniel," I object.

"You are more than welcome to call him and tell him that, but he takes care of his people," he says. "When Josh and his wife lost their baby, he paid for everything and paid his salary for a few months so he could be with his wife. That's just who he is."

"Right now, I need to heal. I'd like to be able to take more than two steps without being in pain before I think about anything else," I say.

"May I ask what your injuries were?" Allison asks.

"Oh yeah. I don't think I told you either, Mildred," I say, and she shakes her head. "I have tearing... well, wherever you can imagine. My cervix apparently is pretty bruised, and I have a concussion. They got me on a lot of antibiotics for some stuff that they did, but also to ward off anything they might've given me. I'll have to go and get tested a few more times before I'm actually in the clear but they think I'm fine."

"Did you get stitches?" Allison asks. "I'm sorry for all the questions. I'm a physician's assistant, so I'm just curious."

"It's okay, and no. They said it was just going to hurt me worse if they did stitches, so it was easier just to let it heal on its own," I explain.

"That makes sense," she says with a nod of her head. "Did they give you emergency contraceptive?"

"Like plan B?" Daniel asks her.

"Yeah," I say. "I have a birth control implant, but they gave it to me just in case."

"I'm at a loss for words, Lila," Daniel says. "Please understand that we are here for you, okay?"

"I appreciate that," I say. "I just need to be alone for a while. I can only tolerate people for so long, but Mildred is going to keep an eye on me. Probably to make sure I don't hang myself."

"I wouldn't think there would be many places to hang yourself in a motel room," Daniel says, and I smile. "Go rest, Lila. Text me where you are, and I'll drop your laptop off. Don't stress out about it though. Tell me when you're ready to come back to work, and we will ease you back into the office."

"Thank you." I say with a sigh.

"It's going to get dark soon. Let's get you back," Mildred says as she stands. I try to stand but pain shoots through my belly and I wince.

"Don't. Let someone help you up," Daniel says as he offers me his hand. He helps me stand and holds onto me for a moment to make sure I'm steady.

"I hate this," I mutter.

"I know," Daniel says. "We will walk you two back to your car before I go grab the laptop. I'll do it tonight, so we can get it out of the way, and I don't bother you."

I sit on the motel bed while the TV plays something random. I'm watching, but I'm not absorbing anything that's on the screen. Mildred dropped me off then went and practically cleared out a dollar store of all their snacks and candy before bringing it back to me.

I think I might just stay here rather than living in my car. It's small and I have everything I need. I can get an electric camping stove and a few dishes. It's pretty clean and the staff seems nice. It would be cheaper to stay here than to get an apartment, so why not? I will admit it's comical that my parents are millionaires, yet their daughter is living in a rundown motel.

There is a knock at the door and at first I panic until I remember that Daniel said he was going to come by. I check out of the little peep hole to make sure before I open the door. "Hey," I say when I open it.

"Hey," Daniel smiles.

"Come in. There are hookers out there," I say as I step to the side, and he laughs. "You think it's funny, but the front desk thinks that I'm a hooker."

"This place isn't nearly nice enough for a high-class lady," he jokes as he sets my laptop on the small desk.

"Oh, right because the victim with a torn perineum is exactly what people are looking for these days," I say.

"People are into weird shit these days," he laughs.

"Thanks for not looking at me like I'm insane when I make jokes like that," I say as I sit on the bed and lay back.

"I'd like to think the dark humor is healing," Daniel says as he sits beside me and lays back with me. "How are you, for real?"

"Not good," I say honestly. "I've never been suicidal, but I think I've come up with every way possible to kill myself in this hotel room."

"Do you actually want to die?"

"No, I just want to feel something other than pain," I say.

"Like what? Happiness? Rage?"

"In control," I admit. "I feel like I'm not in control of my life right now and it's as though everyone else is making decisions for me. Decisions on my body, my home, my relationships... I just want to be the one in control of those things again."

"You are in control of those things," Daniel says as he rolls to his side to prop up on his elbow and look at me.

"How would your wife feel about you lying in bed with another woman?" I ask.

"Well, considering she's with her boyfriend right now, I'm gonna say that she's not really gonna give a shit," he laughs.

"Either you're getting cheated on or you have an open relationship," I say, and he laughs.

"Open relationship. Poly specifically," he says. "You diverted from what I said."

"I don't know how to respond. I don't see how I'm in control of those things. I'm too traumatized to work. I was forced out of my home so now I live in some motel. The only two people on the planet that seem to give a fuck about me is an old lady and my boss."

"You left your relationship when you felt you were not getting the respect you deserved. You left your home when you didn't feel welcome and found yourself a place where you were safe and comfortable. You have autonomy over your body. No one gets to tell you what to do," he says softly.

I roll on to my side and prop myself with my arm to find Daniel watching me closely. "Stop looking at me like that," I laugh.

"Like what?"

"That," I say. "Like you're interested."

"I *am* interested in making you feel something other than pain, but not while you're hurting," he says carefully.

"Fuck," I sigh and close my eyes.

"What?" he asks. I open my eyes again and he's smirking. I don't realize what I'm doing until it's too late. When I press my lips to his, he cups my cheek. The realization washes over me, and I pull away to lay on my back as I cover my face with my hands.

"I'm so sorry. I shouldn't have done that," I say, shocked at myself.

"It's okay," he says, I can hear the smile in his voice. "Did it feel natural?"

"Yeah," I admit.

"Then don't worry about it," he says as he rolls me back onto my side to look at him.

"I'll want to keep going," I say. "What the fuck is wrong with me?" I try to move away, but he pulls me closer and traces his thumb along my jawline.

"Lila, you endured something awful, and now you're desperately trying to find your way. There is no wrong way to deal with this, hun," he says. "I'll admit, I'm not really sure what it is you want to do. Also, I want to note that none of this was my intention."

"I know," I say. "You look like a scolded puppy right now."

"I don't know if I should be offended or not," he laughs.

"You just look like you feel guilty," I smile.

"I don't want you to think that..."

"I know, Daniel," I say. "I don't think you could be forceful if you tried."

"Never know," he grins.

"Ever seen those videos of puppies growling and slinging around toys but don't actually do damage?" I ask and his mouth falls open in shock, making me laugh.

"That was rude," he laughs with me. "I'm actually offended. I am definitely the dominate one."

"If you have to say it, it's probably not true," I add.

I sit up and face him as I pull my legs underneath me to sit on my knees. Daniel moves to lie back and tucks his hand behind his head.

Daniel is a handsome man. He's in his mid-thirties with a lean body. I think he is a runner, so that makes sense. He's a wonderful friend, but he's not someone

I would have a relationship with, even without the trauma. I'm dying to know what he sounds like when he gets his dick sucked though.

"What's on your mind?" he asks.

"Wondering if you'll panic if I do to you what I wanna do," I smile.

"Unless it involves bodily harm, I think I'll be okay," he says. "You seem like the type that would think that kissing with tongue is second base."

"Asshole," I laugh. "Wanna see what I think second base is?"

"Based on the look in your eyes, I think I know," he says, watching me closely.

"All I ask is you don't touch me, okay?" I ask.

"Can I ask why you want to?" he asks.

"Curiosity, but I also want to know if I can do it without melting down. I think mostly... the thought of making decisions like that makes the memories go away."

"As long as you don't feel some obligation to it," he says.

"I don't," I say as I move my hands to undo his belt. My mind is clear and nonc of the panic washes in as I unzip his pants and free his cock. He's big, which is surprising. I don't know why I pictured him having a small dick, but he is far from it. He is thick too, which is even better.

I am thankful that my rapists were on the smaller side. Eight of them with a dick like this would have been a surefire way to kill me.

I grip the base of his cock and lean down to swirl my tongue around the head, collecting the drops of precum from the tip. "Jesus, Lila," Daniel groans and tightens his hands into fists, no doubt trying to keep himself from grabbing me by the hair. I start sucking on the head of his cock and watching his eyes roll back in his head, only fuels my desire to make him come.

When I take him down my throat and hollow my cheeks to suck him, he moans. He touches the back of my head but immediately pulls away. I can tell he is struggling and it's distracting him, so I simply grab his wrists and pin them to his sides. "Fuck, you take my cock so well. God, yes. Just like that."

I am bobbing on his cock, sucking him as hard as I can. The more pleasure I cause him, the more distant the memories become. I move one hand to cup his balls and when I gently squeeze, he fists my hair. I expect myself to panic, but I don't. I keep squeezing and massaging his balls as I suck on him like my life depends on it and eventually let go of his other wrist. He starts to push his hips up to meet my throat and eventually this results in him throat fucking me. I catch myself moaning as he takes his pleasure, which only gives him more pleasure when the vibrations of my voice travel through his cock. Who knew being used could be so much fun.

"Fuck, good girl. Swallow me. God, yes. Yes, just like that. Oh fuck, Lila," he moans as he pushes his cock to the back of my throat. I continue to suck as I drink him down, satisfied with what I have accomplished.

I feel invigorated. The trauma is there. It's still lurking in the back of my head, but it doesn't hurt so damn bad. This is the happiest I've felt since before that man grabbed me on the sidewalk. I know this high will wear off, but I don't care. I'll enjoy it while I can.

"Fuck, I'm sorry," he says almost immediately.

"It's alright," I say.

"Lila, I..."

"Shh. Stop," I say. "It's okay. I could have stopped if it bothered me. That was actually kind of hot, so good job. I think."

"Jesus, you're good at that," he sighs and runs his hands down his face.

"Yeah, you learn a thing or two when you get face fucked until you puke," I say as I move to lie on the bed.

"Aw, you ruined it," he groans, and I can't help but laugh. "You are a twisted little girl, Lila." Daniel rolls to face me.

"Is that good or bad?" I ask.

"It's wonderful," he says with a smile. "You're going to make a man very happy one day."

"I can think of at least nine that I made happy on Friday night," I say, and he shakes his head at me. "Sorry, I'll stop now. Thank you."

"For what? I think I should be thanking you, Lila," he laughs.

"For going along with my... psychosis," I say.

"First of all, you are coping with a trauma. You are not crazy and there is absolutely nothing wrong with how you are choosing to heal," he says. "Do you regret it?"

"No," I say. "It was... nice. I cleared my mind. I know it won't fix the problem, but it makes breathing manageable."

"Well, I'm glad it was enjoyable for you," he says.

"More than I expected," I laugh, then yawn.

"I'll go so you can sleep," he says.

"Okay," I say. "I can't promise that I'll work any time soon."

"Don't worry about that," he says as he sits up. "Just focus on healing."

"That can't happen again," I say. "I get attached to people who are sweet to me, and that's a dangerous road to go down when I am teetering on the edge."

"I know," he says as he squats down in front of me to take my hands. "Lila, honey... you're still navigating through this. You will heal. You will never forget, but you will heal."

"We'll see," I say.

"You have my number. Call me if you need me. I mean that," he says as he stands up. "Day or night, I will answer."

"Thank you, Daniel," I say with a sigh.

I walk him to the door where we say our goodbyes. I shut myself in and lock the deadbolt before hooking the chain lock. I sigh and lean against the door, looking around my room. "Home sweet home," I mutter sarcastically.

I gather what I need to take a shower and head into the bathroom, avoiding the mirror. I go through the same process of letting the water get as hot as possible before stepping in. As I wash my body and I see the bruises, I can feel myself slip out of the high that I created with Daniel and come crashing down into my self-despair.

Once the tears start, I can't stop them. It was nice to pretend I was okay for a moment, but now I am back in reality. The weight of the whiplash I have taken on in the last three days is more than I can handle right now. I slide down the shower wall and sit under the scalding water jetting down on me from the shower head. My breathing comes in ragged gasps, the sobs wracking my body with each shuddering exhale. The echoes of my cries reverberate off the tiled walls. It's like a symphony of anguish and despair that fills the room but like it did in the abandoned building when I was surrounded by those men. This emotional pain feels like I'm drowning, suffocating beneath the weight of the memories that threaten to consume me. Its relentlessness is a constant reminder of the horrors I endured at the hands of those men. Their faces blur together in my mind. They are just nameless, faceless monsters lurking in the shadows of my memories. I can still feel their hands on my skin, their cruel laughter ringing in my ears as they tore my world apart.

Being with Daniel gave me momentary solace but as the water washes away the remnants of my tears, I am left feeling raw and exposed, stripped bare of the armor I built around myself for years. Armor that taught me to be so brave as to assume that bad things happened to other people, not me. I feared what I didn't understand, but I got it now. I know what lies beyond the light and after having walked through the depths of Hell, the only thing I fear is living.

Chapter Four

Nash

I AM SITTING ON the couch with my head back when I hear my front door open. The dainty footsteps tell me that it's Mildred, but the second, heavier set of steps tell me someone else is with her, I open my eyes and I'm confused. "Daniel?" I ask.

"Hey, man," he sighs.

"What's wrong? How do you know Mildred?" I ask. Based on the look on Mildred's face, something bad happened. I've never seen her not smiling.

"You know the new engineer I hired a few months ago? She did her master's in four years," he says.

"Yeah. Lila Monroe. Why?" I ask and look at Mildred. "Do you know Lila or something?"

"I do now," she says vaguely.

"Someone needs to explain, because I don't have much patience today," I say. I can't get those screams out of my head. It's like a constant reminder that I need to help her.

"She was gang raped, Nash," Mildred says bluntly. "Around one in the morning on Saturday."

"Was it near the funeral home?" I ask, sitting up.

"Yeah," she says. "How'd you know that?"

"I was outside getting some air after putting some bodies in for the prison," I say. "I heard someone screaming, I just didn't know where it was coming from."

"That was her," Daniel says.

"Dear God. Is she ?" I ask. Now I really feel like an ass. I've never met her, but knowing I jerked off to her getting gang raped makes me feel some kind of way.

"Physically, yeah. She got lucky," Mildred says. "She has some tearing and a concussion. But mentally... not at all."

"She called me and asked me to meet her today. Me and Alli met her, and she quit."

"What?" I ask. "Why?"

"Well, I have her talked out of it for now. I told her to take as much time as she needs, and her job will be there when she's ready. She was accepting of that but... she's lost everything, Nash. She's living in a motel."

"The night she was raped, her boyfriend and best friend ditched her downtown so they could go back to the apartment they all shared to have sex. Apparently, she heard something over the phone and decided to walk home to try and catch them. She was dragged into that old flower shop where she was brutally raped by eight men. They left her there for dead. I ended up finding her about twelve hours later. But... her ex owed this gang money, and they went after her." Mildred says.

"Oh... shit," I say. "They think she's dead."

"Mhmm. She saw all of them, Nash. If they find out she's alive..."

"They'll come after her again," I sigh. "Why are you telling me this and not the cops?

"Daniel knows," Mildred says vaguely.

"Did you..."

"No. He just kind of put it together but it's unconfirmed."

"What is it you think you know?" I ask Daniel.

"Well... I know you own a funeral home and crematorium," he says. "I know you hate rapists and wife beaters. I know you have encountered a few that have then gone on to turn up missing."

"So?" I ask.

"I think you are killing these fuckers and burning their bodies. The only reason I have put this together is because I work so closely with you, so... I doubt anyone else has put it together."

"Sit," I say as I point to the seat across from me. His aura is a bright white as always. He's a good guy. I don't think he's capable of hurting someone, but he seems to feel guilty about something.

"Nash, I swear to God..."

"Stop," I say. "Do you understand why I do what I do?"

"No, but they deserve it, so I don't really care if it's to sacrifice them to the flying spaghetti monster," he says matter-of-factly.

"In pasta we trust," Mildred chuckles to herself. I smile and shake my head.

"Back to Lila for a second. Where is she now?"

"Willard's Motel," Daniel says. "Room 120."

"Yeah, it's clean. I brought a bunch of easy things for her to eat," Mildred says.

"She said there are hookers, and they think she's one, but it doesn't seem seedy or anything," Daniel adds.

"Oh, you took her laptop to her last night?" Mildred asks him. "How was she?"

"Uh... odd," he says slowly.

"Is she okay?" Mildred asks.

"Yeah... I mean... I don't know," he says. He keeps glancing at me, and I understand why he feels guilty.

"What happened?" I ask, but he doesn't say anything. "The only thing I would get mad at you for is if you forced her to do anything or if you fucked her while she's injured."

"She..." he starts to say but stops.

"Out with it, Daniel," I sigh.

"She was... insistent on wanting to give me head," he says carefully.

"You didn't turn her down, did you?" Mildred says before I have the chance to react.

"No," he says. "She started everything and just requested that I didn't touch her but..."

"But you did?" I ask.

"Yeah. At first, I just had my hand on her head but..."

"I understand," I say. "Did she get upset?"

"No. That's what's odd about it. She moaned when I got a bit too carried away," he says. "She said over and over that it was fine, and she enjoyed it but..."

"You think you violated her," Mildred finishes and he nods. "Baby... survivors of sexual assault often turn to consensual sex to cope. Hypersexuality is not a big deal as long as she isn't taking risks. As far as you getting rough with her, you don't know what she's into consensually. She also could have a forced sex kink. It's also called consensual non-consent. Over sixty percent of survivors have this kink. It is very normal and healthy. It shows that she trusts you."

"Alli know?" I ask.

"Yeah, I called her when I left. She said the same thing Mildred said," he says.

"Then relax," I say. "Now… what exactly do you want me to do?"

"You are the only one who can help her," Mildred says. "She's hardly hanging on."

"I will happily find the men who did this to her, but I need her to trust me enough to go into detail. These men will be naturally well hidden. If she's alive, they aren't going to go boasting about it. It's going to be hard to find them. Once they get word that I know… let's just say that I am known on the street, but no one knows who I am or where these people disappear to… but they know why."

They call me "The Wraith". They know why I'm going to kill them, because I tell them on the dark web, but they don't know who I am or when I'll show up. They just know that once I've made you my target… it's only a matter of time. No one suspects a well-respected billionaire, who runs his adoptive father's funeral home on the side, of vicious murders. They all beg for their lives in the end. I will make it my life mission to hunt these men down and let her watch as I drain the life out of each and every one of them. I will take their life and give it to her as a promise of hope for our happiness. I will free her of this pain, but I need to catch my little butterfly first. Before I can catch her, I need to watch her.

"I'll watch her for a week or two to get a feel for who she is and how exactly she is coping before I approach her," I say. "If she's suicidal, we all need to be watching her. If there is any chance that these men are going to come after her again, she needs to have someone near her at all times, doesn't matter if she knows or not. Just don't scare the poor woman."

"You mean stalk her?" Daniel asks.

"Basically," I shrug. "She's going to fake a smile to make you all feel like she's okay. She wanted to quit in fear of being a burden, thinking we would be bothered by her trauma and need for space. The only way I will know how to help her is if I know just how much she wants to die."

"How exactly are you going to help though?" Daniel asks.

"You really want to know?" I ask, glancing at Mildred.

"Yeah, I think," he says.

"I'm going to make her beg for her life," I say simply. "People don't realize how much they want to live until they're about to die, and she will be no different."

"So, you're going to brutalize an already brutalized woman and expect her to want to live?" he snaps. He's protective of her. I like that. I don't see him as a threat to my butterfly or how I will make her love me, but she has a friend. I'm glad she has him.

"No, Daniel," I say. "I might cause her pain, but she will never be in any real danger. I will only induce the feeling of death. I will push her, but I will get her permission before I ever lay a hand on her."

"How?" he frowns.

"Simple... she wants to die... and I want to kill. It's a win-win situation, except in the end, she will still be very much alive."

One Week Later

I am sitting at a table in the back of the bar next to Lila's motel drinking a beer while I watch a man talk to her. He's not being aggressive, mostly because she is giving in to everything he says. She is following his lead and it's put her from sitting alone with her fruity drink to sitting in his lap in a matter of minutes.

I can see it in her pretty blue eyes that she wants him to go away, but she gives no resistance and fawns for a man who isn't actually pushy. She's afraid of saying no, like as if she does, she might get hurt again. She can't get hurt if she doesn't say no, so now she is following him into the men's restroom.

I sigh heavily and stand. I already know he will have her bent over the counter by the time I get in there. As long as he isn't hurting her and he's wearing a condom, I won't interfere. I have no place to tell her what to do with her body. She is finding her place in this world again, but she's looking in all the wrong places. She deserves the best things life has to offer, but she's looking in sketchy bars beneath a man who is definitely on cocaine right now.

I pull my mask from the inside pocket of my trench coat and slip it on before walking into the bathroom. Right away I hear the sounds of skin on skin slapping. When I round the corner, I see that he has her bent at the waist. She is resting her weight on her elbows. He is behind her with his hands gripping her hips. I see the condom wrapper on the counter as he pounds into her pussy. She makes little grunts and moans that tell me she is not being hurt.

I lean against the wall and watch for a moment before flipping the lock. The man doesn't notice, but her eyes fly open and immediately land on me as I pull my cock out. I grip the base and start stroking myself as she stares at me.

"You like what you see, baby?" she says to me, but the man responds.

"Fuck yeah, girl. Fuck you're so tight," he groans.

The sights and sounds around me intensify my arousal and keep my eyes fixed on hers. Her sweet moans and the slap of their flesh against each other fill the air, and I match their rhythm with my own strokes, imagining myself as the one fucking her. I lose myself in the erotic symphony, my body responding to all of the sensations. For a few moments, I am no longer just an observer, but a part of this. I can see it on her face that she is imagining I am the one deep inside of her. She can't take her eyes off me as he pumps away. She reaches between her legs and starts to rub her clit, desperate to feel something. Anything. My heart races, my breaths shallow, and my hand moves faster, the pleasure building within me like a tidal wave. Just as I am about to come, I stop. My come is meant for my little butterfly now. The only place it will be going is inside of her.

When I tuck my painfully hard cock away, she whines and gives up on touching herself. She lost her orgasm because I stopped. Interesting.

The man groans and pumps into her as he finishes. As he pulls out, I step into one of the stalls, so he doesn't see me.

"Uh, thanks for that," the man says.

"Mhmm," she says dismissively. "Have a good night."

"Uh… you too," he says, confused. "Not going to ask to see me again?"

"Do you want to see me again?" she asks.

"Well, no I don't really date," he says. "You just don't seem like the girl to get fucked and not ask for a number."

"Well, I'm glad I'm your first innocent-looking whore. You can go now, I'm just going to clean up." The man leaves the bathroom without another word, still likely confused as fuck.

I step out and watch as she fixes her dress and touches up her makeup. I know she knows I'm here. She glances up at me but doesn't flinch when she finds that I am inches away. This mask has made grown men piss themselves, but not my little butterfly. No… she doesn't fear death. She walked along the edge of Hell, begging to be dragged under. She knows that with life there is pain. She's tired of the pain. She has no energy left to weather the storm of emotions that it brings on. Facing the emotions is what scares her. The pain is what will set her free. My little butterfly will soon be free.

"Are you just going to stare at me?" she asks as she turns to me. When I don't say anything, she rolls her eyes and goes to step past me. Right as she gets to my side, I catch her with my hand wrapped around her dainty little throat and push her back against the wall.

Her breathing hitches for a moment before going shallow. Her eyes widen and her pupils dilate, but she says nothing. She doesn't move an inch. "Oh, how easy it would be to snap this pretty little neck, butterfly," I say with a soft tone.

"Then do it," Lila says seriously.

"You'd love that, wouldn't you, Lila?" I ask. I chuckle when the confusion sweeps across her face. "You'd love it if I tightened my grip while I fucked you."

"Either do something or fuck off," she says simply. Instead of responding, I tighten my grip just enough that it turns her skin a beautiful shade of pink as she struggles to breathe. I slide my other hand up her dress and into her lace panties.

"Oh, sweet butterfly. Is this all for me?" I ask when I find that her cunt is dripping for me. I start to rub her clit and her eyes roll back as she moans. I pinch and rub her pussy until she is nearly convulsing. She is moaning loudly, but right as she starts to peak, I stop.

"You don't get to come, my love. You've been naughty," I growl. "Be a good girl and next time I'll let you come. Understood?"

"Yes," she says softly.

"Yes, what?"

"Yes, sir," she corrects.

"Go back to your motel room and lock the door," I command.

"Yes, sir."

Chapter Five

Lila

One Week Later

EVERY TIME I FUCK someone, he's there. I can always count on him and that mask joining me after and making me come until I can't remember my name. He doesn't fuck me though. I should start calling him the magical masked finger man, because Lord have mercy is he amazing with his hands.

My masked lover looks as though he peeled the flesh from a rotting clown and stapled it to a hockey mask. It's horrific and bloody. The skin is this disgusting hue of a sickly gray with hints of blue and green mottling the flesh. The mouth is a toothless gash, while the eyes are hollowed sockets that have sunken in, and deep within the depths of the darkness I can see the bright blue that makes up his eyes. I should be terrified of this man, but I just want him to fuck me already. No one else has been able to make me come or take away the pain like he can with just his hands. God, I never thought someone stalking me would be so fucking hot, but here we are. I fuck the others because it's easier than telling them no, but this man... I will never say no to him. Not because I can't or don't know how, I just want everything he has to offer me. His aura is a ghostly, silver-gray with a muted radiance that adds depth to its hue. I sense that he is vibrant underneath all of the darkness and I want nothing more than to tunnel my way into his soul where I can rest comfortably knowing I am surrounded by him. I'm sure this mask is an image directly from someone's nightmare, but not mine. No. This man will set me free.

Mildred and Daniel take turns having dinner with me every night. They both call me every day. I end up texting with them for most of the day. Even Allison texts me. I felt bad after blowing her husband, so I asked Daniel for her number. I tried to apologize, but she asked me not to. She said that he knows where their boundaries lie, and she knows he will never cross them. They can each have their fun and remain married. They are each other's priority. I respect that they can be so comfortable with that dynamic.

Allison is the one who knows I've been fucking everything that breathes in my direction. I wish I was joking, but I'm not. It's like a compulsion. If a man shows any interest, I fold like a house of cards in an earthquake. I always have condoms with me, and I never bring anyone to my motel room. Every night I sit alone in the shower and sob, processing that pain repeatedly. The downfall from that post-sex high is just as rough now as it was the first time.

The first time I had sex after the rape, it was with some random guy last week. That's the first time the masked man showed up too. Luckily the guy wasn't huge because I was still sore. My stalker touched me for the first time but didn't let me come. He brought me right to the edge, called me naughty, then disappeared like a ghost. I can tell he doesn't like when I'm with these men, but he doesn't stop them. He just watches from a distance.

I eat at night when I'm all alone. I eat way too much and to the point that I make myself sick. When I don't, I think about suicide. If I'm fucking or eating, none of it hurts. The intrusive thoughts about all the different ways I can end my life don't sneak their way in. I don't keep down most of the food I eat, so I'm losing weight. I don't know how I feel about that, but at least I'm thinner.

I need to get out of this room. I need a few things from the store, so I use it as an excuse to leave. I could take my car to the grocery store, but I'm going to walk. I'm stuck in my head today so the fresh air will be good for me, I think.

I step out of my motel room and walk through the parking lot to the sidewalk. "Hey... girl," a man calls out. I turn to see it's the motel manager.

"Hey," I say tentatively. The man is in his mid-forties. He's a bit sleazy looking, but I think it's just how he's dressed. He has khaki shorts on and a floral print, button up shirt with a few buttons at the top unhooked to reveal his chest hair. He has a gold chain around his neck and sunglasses on his head.

"You didn't pay for last week," he says.

"Yeah, I did. I put cash in an envelope in the drop box like you told me to," I say.

"Well, I didn't get it," he says. "Late fee doubles it."

"What? That's ridiculous," I frown.

"That's the rules, girl. So, are you gonna pay or are you gonna take your clients somewhere else?"

"Jesus Christ... I'm not a hooker. How many times do I have to say that?" I say with an attitude.

"Fine," he smirks. "Get your shit and get out of my motel." He abruptly turns and walks back into the office, leaving me standing in the parking lot.

"What? I never said I wouldn't pay. Just tell me how much it is," I say, following him into the office.

"For you?" he says, turning to face me. "A thousand."

"What?! That's fucking stupid. That's four times what I pay. You can't do that," I complain.

"I can and I am," he says. "You either shut that door and come over here or you pay a thousand bucks a week."

"Fuck," I sigh.

"What's it gonna be, Layla?" he asks.

"It's Lila," I say quietly as he walks closer, greedily scanning my body.

"It's whatever I want it to be, whore," he says in my ear. "Lift that little dress and bend over for me and we'll call it even, huh?"

My mind is racing, and I know I don't have a choice. Even if I say no and get kicked out of here, he's still going to fuck me. I can see it on his face. I can either fight him and get fucked raw or just let him take what he wants, and I can get him to wear a condom. Letting him fuck me once a week isn't all bad. He looks like he will be quick.

"What's it gonna be, whore?" he asks, licking my cheek.

"Fine," I say so quietly that I am barely audible.

"Shut the door and come here," he says as he walks to his desk. I turn and go to the door and see my masked man in the parking lot. I have tears running down my cheeks and he looks pissed. He has a phone in his hand and his body is tense. If he grips that phone any harder, it's going to shatter.

I shut the door and turn to the desk. He has an evil smirk on his face as he unhooks his belt. My body is trembling, and I can hardly hold my own weight as I walk over to stand in front of him.

"Hands on the desk, little slut," he says as he roughly turns me around.

"Please wear a condom," I say with a shaky voice.

"Of course. I don't want to catch whatever you have picked up fucking all those men at the bar," he says in my ear before biting my neck. I don't even try to hold back my tears as he pulls my underwear down my thighs and pushes me to lay over his desk. He keeps his hand between my shoulder blades so if I fight, he has leverage. I don't fight though. I lay there and take it.

I hear him tear open a condom before he spits in his hand and wipes his saliva on his dick. When will men realize that spit is not lube?

As soon as he pushes into me, I know he's going to hurt me if I fight him. He is big enough to push against my cervix. Luckily, he starts slow. The more I cry the faster he fucks me. I keep still, even when he takes his hand off my back to roughly grip my waist with his disgusting hands.

"Goddamn, such a tight little whore," he grunts out. "Let's see how tight this fat ass is. I love the way you cry."

My cries instantly turned to sobs when I hear the cap of the bottle pop open. He drips the lube on my ass before pulling out and swirling his dick on my tight hole. I'm trying to be as relaxed as I can because I know what he's about to do. No matter how many times I tell myself to just relax it doesn't help. It still surprises me, and I still scream. He chuckles right before he rams his dick in me. In one swift stroke, he buries himself to the hilt and I scream through gritted teeth. He quickly covers my mouth before he starts to thrust rapidly into me.

When I stop screaming, he fists my hair and yanks my head back as I sob. He pulls me up to my hands and rocks my body against the desk. "Come for me, bitch," he growls and starts roughly rubbing, pinching, and pulling at my clit. My body responds to his abuse, and I am quickly transported to another dimension. I see the masked man outside. He's moved into view now. Normally he jerks off when he watches me get railed, but not this time. This time I was forced, and he doesn't seem to like when men get aggressive with me.

I focus on my masked stalker and imagine that he is the one railing me into this desk right now. When I picture him, I can relax and let my body do what is natural. I know it's only responding to what the man is doing to me. My body is only doing its job. It doesn't understand that I don't want to come but when that fiery pressure builds in my belly, I'm instantly nauseous. It's too late though. A weak orgasm ripples through me and the man inside of me is dragged into his own release when my body tenses around his dick.

"Come back next week with two fifty and I'll see how well my little whore sucks cock," he says. He slaps me on the ass and pushes me away from his desk. I stumble but catch myself before pulling my underwear back up and running out of the office.

I abandon the idea of going to the store and run back to my room. I'm still sobbing when I get in. I go to shut the door but a boot wedged in the doorway prevents it from shutting. I look up and through my teary haze, I see my masked man. I leave him standing there and turn to go to the bathroom.

I need to get the feeling of him off my skin. I turn the shower on as hot as it will go when I hear the lock on my door, followed by heavy footsteps toward me. I ignore him and strip off my clothes and step into the scalding water. It instantly takes my breath away and I slide down the shower wall and pull my knees to my chest.

"Butterfly," he says softly.

"Please don't do it," I cry. "I can't handle it right now."

"I'm not," he says as he slowly moves closer. "Stand and let me help." He holds his hand out and it takes me a second, but I let him pull me up.

"What are you going to do?" I ask. I see him in such a positive light, and I really hope he's not about to ruin that image for me.

"I'm going to wash the dead man off of my butterfly," he says. I furrow my brow at him in confusion.

"What do you mean by dead man? You don't mean..."

"Anyone who hurts my butterfly dies, Lila," he says, tilting my chin up so I look at him. He has gorgeous blue eyes. They shimmer in the artificial light of the bathroom. I get lost in his gaze for a moment, wondering what he looks like.

"He's dead?" I ask.

"No, but soon," he says.

"What's your name?" I ask.

"Wraith," he says.

"Bet that was fun to spell in kindergarten," I joke, and he chuckles. "Will I ever get to know who you really are?"

"When the time is right, I'll make you mine. Until then, I'll be watching... protecting you."

"If I'm yours, why do you let those men have sex with me?" I ask. My voice is quiet. I feel so small next to him but somehow, I feel safe.

"Because it's your body, Lila," he says. "You are in control of what happens to your body. The moment someone does something you don't want, I'll slit their fucking throat."

"Why would you do that for me? You don't know me."

"I do know you," he says, cupping my face with his large hand. "I know you're hoping I'll kill you. You look for danger and you pray that it will take you out. Maybe one of the men you fuck will strangle you. Maybe you'll walk down the wrong alley, and someone will rape and kill you."

"I don't look for rape," I frown.

"No, but you look for any situation that might lead you to your death," he says. "Tell me I'm wrong."

"You're wrong, I don't want to..." I start to say but I get cut off when he grabs me by the throat and pins me to the shower wall.

"Then fight me," he growls in my ear.

I don't want to fight. He's right... maybe I do look for danger in hopes of getting killed. I'm too much of a pansy to do it myself so I'm hoping someone else will do it for me.

I am hyper aware of the ache between my legs as he chokes me. I can't draw in a breath and my vision is filled with stars. Every time my vision starts to tunnel, he lets up just enough so that I don't pass out. When he does this, I whimper. Fuck, what is he doing to my body?

"My sweet little butterfly," he says. "Does this turn you on? Do you like the idea of dying that much?" I nod and whimper when he lets up and I suck in oxygen.

"Please," I whisper.

"What is it, butterfly?"

"Please... please just kill me... I know you have killed others. I can sense it in your aura. Please kill me. I don't want to be here anymore. I'm sick of living. I can't handle this pain anymore."

"I will make you beg me to let you live."

"I don't want to live," I frown.

"Then if you don't beg to live... you'll die. You will take your last breath with me buried in your sweet little cunt," he says softly. His filthy words have my pussy aching to be filled and pounded. It's more than a want. I need him.

Wraith begins to wash my body, not caring that he is getting water on himself. He doesn't seem to mind the hot water and I don't mind how he touches me. I love that he doesn't even attempt anything sexual. He cleanses every inch of my body, but it's as if he is a caretaker, not the man who said he'd kill me while he fucked my dying body. I've never had someone take care of me. Jeff sure as fuck never did anything like this. This man hardly knows me, and he is taking better care of me than Jeff did in eight years.

I was fourteen when I met Jeff. He was twenty and he made me feel like the prettiest girl ever. He doted on me and the things we did were definitely illegal. He took my virginity the first time we hung out at his apartment and as long as I kept coming back to let him fuck me, he kept giving me attention. Eventually, things turned into a full-fledged relationship where we ended up moving in together when I turned eighteen. Jessika moved in two years later, which is when they started fucking, apparently.

When Wraith is done washing my body, he shuts the water off and dries me. I'm exhausted now, so when he walks me into the bedroom and gets me dressed,

I sigh in relief. Part of me wishes that he would just hold me down and fuck me, but I don't think I can handle that right now without getting triggered. He pulls the covers back and has me lie down before he moves to lay behind me. I am snuggled under the covers when he pulls his mask off and lays it on my hip.

"You trust me enough for that?" I ask softly. I am facing away from him as he pulls me closer. I can feel his breath on the back of my neck and a soft tickle of his beard.

"Yes, Butterfly. I trust you," he says, kissing my shoulder. "I give you the same amount of trust that you give me."

"I feel like the whole world is against me except you," I say. "Daniel and Mildred mean well, but they don't understand what I went through... but you do."

"I do understand... I wish I didn't. I wish neither of us understood, but this is the hand we were dealt in life."

"Being alive is exhausting," I mumble.

"Sleep, my sweet butterfly. Tomorrow is a new day," he says. I snuggle in closer to him and settle into the mattress. It doesn't take me long to drift away into my dreams. For the first time since before the rape, I dream of happier days.

Chapter Six

Nash

WHEN LILA'S BREATHING EVENS out, I slowly get up and slip my mask back on before rounding the bed to look at her. She calmed down a lot once I started taking care of her. I think if that loser, Jeff, had done that from the beginning she might not have fallen as far as she has. I will piece her back together and she will go on to live a happier life with me than she ever would have with him.

The fucker is lucky I haven't killed him. He preyed on her at fourteen when he was twenty. A grown man has no business being with a girl hardly old enough to menstruate. If she had been seventeen or eighteen, okay fine. But she was a freshman in high school while he was a sophomore in college. Where were her parents when this happened? I know they are alive, but living in England, however you'd think they would have protected their child. Obviously, teens will always find a way to get into things they shouldn't, with or without permission, but I'm thinking they just didn't give a fuck enough to care.

Lila's soul is beautiful. Watching her sleep and seeing her truly relaxed because of my presence triggers something inside of me. I never thought love was meant for me until I met her... she's so broken... she's perfect. Why do I need perfection when I am far from it myself? No one is perfect but she is perfect for me and I for her. That I am sure of.

My butterfly is sleeping so peacefully. Her soft moans and gentle breathing fill the room, and I can't help but be captivated by her beauty. I gently pull the covers back to reveal her body. I trace my fingers along the delicate curves. As I run my hand across her chest, I can feel the warmth of her body against mine, her heart beating in steady rhythm. My pants grow tight and with each breath, the desire within me becomes more intense.

I free my cock from the confines of my jeans, and I stroke myself, matching the rhythm of my hand with the rhythm of my thoughts. Lila stirs in her sleep, and I can't resist the temptation any longer. With a sudden urgency, I guide the tip of my cock over the delicate skin of her lips. The sensation is intoxicating, a fusion of pleasure and power that takes my breath away.

As if responding to my touch, Lila's eyes flutter open, her gaze heavy and hazy with sleep. She stares at me, her expression a mix of surprise and curiosity. And then, without a word, she parts her lips, wrapping them around the head of my cock. I shudder at the feeling of her warm mouth enveloping me, her gentle suction sending waves of pleasure through my body. I watch her, mesmerized by the sight of my butterfly in action. I gently push my cock to the back of her throat. She grabs my hips and I expect her to give resistance, but she pulls me closer. I push deeper and slowly start fucking her throat as she moans. Her tongue is rubbing each barbell, I can't help but grip onto the headboard and quicken my pace. I glance back when she moves again, and I see that she has her hand slipped into her panties. She is touching herself while I fuck her mouth. Her moans vibrate around me, this brings out something feral in me. I move my hands to hold her head steady while I move faster. She has hollowed her cheeks sucking me as hard as she can while she rubs her clit faster and faster. Her other hand is gripping my ass for support and the combination of everything is so goddamn erotic and addicting. We are both moaning, desperate to come. As she starts to come, she whimpers and moans as she sucks. Her pleasure easily pulls mine forward and I surrender to the intense pleasure that now consumes me. Lila moves her other hand to my ass and pulls my hips in, taking all of me down her throat.

"Fuck, Lila. Such a good girl," I groan. "Swallow me, baby. Take all of me."

Lila starts to hum in delight and the vibrations make my eyes roll back as I start to come. "You're mine, little butterfly... no one touches you without my permission," I say as I drain myself and she happily drinks me down. She keeps sucking until the sensations are too intense and I pull out of her mouth.

"Thank y..." her words abruptly stop when we hear the jingling of keys outside of her motel door. She instantly pulls the cover over her and moves into the fetal position. We both know it's that prick coming after her again.

"Wraith," she whimpers as she hides her face. I lean down and slip my mask up so I can kiss her on the head.

"Don't worry, Butterfly, he will learn to not hurt what's mine," I say softly. She doesn't say anything, and her body is trembling. "Sleep now, I have a pest to exterminate."

When her body relaxes, I take a step back and she peeks out from under the covers. As soon as I face the door, we hear the key slip into the lock. I get to the door right as it opens, but he freezes when he sees me in my mask.

"Shit," he says as he turns on his heels and bolts.

"Shut and lock the door," I say to Lila as I chase after the cowardly rapist. He's not so big and bad when he has me running him down. Although, I don't know many people who wouldn't shit themselves having a six-foot four man with a dead clown mask on chasing them.

"Come on, Princess. I just wanna talk," I say as I leap for him and take us both to the ground.

"Stop, stop, stop," he begs, but I punch him in the jaw, causing his head to bounce off the pavement perfectly so that his body goes limp.

"Asshole. I fucking hate running in jeans," I mutter as I get off the ground. I turn back to make sure Lila shut the motel door, but I find that she is standing out on the sidewalk in front of her room. She has her robe on now, grinning from ear to ear.

Fuck, I think I'm in love with this woman already.

As I am tying the last knot, the manager of Lila's motel starts to wake. I have him stripped naked, sitting in a metal chair in the center of the room. I bring my victims to the basement of the funeral home because it's soundproof. This room isn't on the official blueprints and the entrance is hidden. The building itself dates to the prohibition era, so I don't doubt that this place was hidden for a reason.

There is a drain in the floor, and everything is lined with stainless steel. I did it this way to make cleanup easier rather than if it were just concrete. I have everything I need down here, but I bring clean coveralls, face shields, and gloves every time. I had extras here thankfully, because I wasn't planning on killing tonight. I haven't hunted since the night Lila was gang raped. I have been so focused on her that I haven't had the urge, until this asshole raped her.

"Morning, fucker." I walk over to the metal table where I have all my tools. I have a small storage area for chemicals I may use, but I haven't gotten there yet. I'm still deciding what I will do to this asshole.

"So... now that I've seen your face... can I know your name?" Lila asks with hesitation in her voice. She understands the significance of her seeing my face as well as her being here. If she's scared, she doesn't show it.

She's surrounded by darkness, but I can still see the bright girl she once was. Before the pain, before the betrayal. That colorful light is fighting to shine through. Her aura is a lackluster shade of gray, like a sky heavy with clouds before a storm. It whispers of shadows and echoes of pain, a silent plea for solace in a world of turmoil. Yet beneath the surface, a quiet resilience lingers, a flicker of hope waiting to be kindled. I know every color of the rainbow is still deep within her soul, begging to be released from its melancholia. I will be what gives her life purpose again. I will let every color bleed out of her to transform her mind into a place of peace. Once I reignite the passion in her soul, I will be her God, her world, and her reason for breathing.

"Nash Sutton," I say with a smirk as I move to stand in front of her with my hands on either side of the table where she is sitting. She is still in that oversize T-shirt, but she has shorts and sandals on now.

"You... you own Papillon Security Management," she says. "You're my boss... Daniel's boss..."

"I am," I say simply. The motel manager, whose name I do not know, is grunting and trying to talk behind his gag, but she and I both ignore him. "Mildred is my adoptive Aunt. She's the sister of the man who adopted me when I was sixteen."

"She's sweet," Lila says. "Does she know..."

"She knows about Wraith. Daniel learned when he and Mildred came to talk to me about you," I explain.

"So, you know what happened?"

"I know it happened. I know I inadvertently heard it happen because I was here, but I do not know the details of what took place," I reassured her. "Even if they knew, which I doubt they do, they would want you to be the one to tell me."

"Oh..." she says looking down at her hands.

"One thing at a time, butterfly," I say, lifting her chin so I can see her pretty blue eyes. I smile when I see fearful tears that she's desperately trying to blink away. I'll be the first to admit that it's a bit fucked up that I am happy she is scared of me, but if she's scared, it means she values her safety. From the moment I heard those screams... I knew she still had fight left in her. No matter what they did to her, she is stronger than they are. She may not know it, but she will survive this.

"What are you going to do to him?" she asks, glancing at the motel manager.

"I am going to flay him, I think," I say.

"You mean..."

"I'm going to skin him," I say as I move over to the table to pick up my boning knife. For flaying meat, a boning knife is typically used. This type of knife has a narrow, pointed blade that is specifically designed for separating the skin from the muscle with precision. The blade is flexible, allowing it to maneuver around the body easily. The sharpness of the blade ensures clean and precise cuts while allowing me to keep control. When skinning someone, you don't want to cut too deep, or they'll die. You want shallow cuts that stay within the layers of skin.

"Shit. That sucks for him," she shrugs.

"If you get sick, there is a trash can over there," I say, pointing to the corner of the room.

"I'll be fine," she says confidently.

"Let's see what our little friend has to say then," I say as I pull the gag off of him.

"*Help*!" he screams. "*Help me!*"

"Are you don-"

"Help!" He screams louder, and Lila giggles.

"The room is concrete and metal, under a brick building. No one can hear you," I deadpan.

"You're a fucking psycho, man!" he screams at me.

"Oh, but raping a woman is okay?" I ask.

"I didn't rape anyone. She never said no," he objects.

"What were you doing coming into her room then?" I ask. "Because I know damn well she didn't invite you. Also, if a woman sobbing while you fuck her is your idea of consent, then you are about to have an even bigger problem."

"All this over some whore?" he shouts. I laugh dryly and glance at Lila before moving to stand in front of the man.

"You see that whore... she's special to me. No one gets to hurt her but me. No one gets to break her... but me. I hacked your camera in your office and watched as you raped her while she cried," I say. "You have one opportunity to tell me what you were going to do when you came to her room."

"I was going to fuck her again, okay? I figured she was asleep or something because she didn't go to the bar."

"But you didn't know I was there. I guess it's a good thing I've been watching her, huh?" I ask. "I'm tired of talking. Let's see you bleed."

I start on his right shoulder and angle the blade so that I can run it parallel with his body. The first cut makes him groan in pain, but when I start to slice down and peel a strip of flesh from his chest, he screams loudly. He begins crying and begging, but I tune out his pleas and keep cutting.

Chapter Seven

Lila

I AM SITTING ON the metal embalming table as I watch Nash work. It's amazing. Hearing this fucker's screams echo off the walls is like listening to my favorite song. It's gruesome and messy, but it's justice. Sometimes justice gets nasty.

I can tell he has done this many times. The way he keeps his hand steady and slowly drags the blade, leaving clean lines that all have a consistent depth. He peels back the skin slowly, exposing the raw muscle slick with blood beneath. There is no doubt that he does this to draw out the pain. "Why did you do it?" Nash asks in a deceivingly calm tone.

"I don't know. Please stop. I swear I won't touch her again, man please," the man sobs.

"Oh, it's too late for that," Nash chuckles.

"Uhm... Nash," I say quietly.

"Yes?" he says, turning his attention to me.

"Can I... I'd really like to be the reason he screams," I say, gaining a bit more confidence. His smile grows wide, almost giddy that I want to partake in the torture of my rapist.

"Yeah," he says. "Grab some gloves. There are coveralls beside you. They'll be big because you are so tiny, but it'll do what it's intended to do."

I nod excitedly before jumping down from the table. I pull on my gloves first before grabbing the coveralls. I end up having to roll the pant legs and the sleeves, but they fit me well enough. "How do I look?" I say as I spin for him.

"Beautiful, Butterfly," he says with a smile.

"You're both sick," the man sobs.

"Is it bad that I don't know his name?" I ask.

"No. Scum doesn't need a name," he says as he steps behind me and places the knife in my hand. "Now... work from left to right in even strips. You can make a small cut to start off so you can have something to grab hold of." Nash explains.

I make a horizontal cut and blood oozes from the fresh wound. One side of his chest is stripped to reveal bands of muscle in multiple spots. I'm surprised he hasn't passed out yet. I'm sure he's in shock at this point. I know partway through my rape with the eight men, I went numb.

"Okay, good. Now, you want to run the blade parallel with his body. Go slow so that you can make sure your cuts are even and they don't go too deep. If they are, he will start bleeding faster, which will result in him dying quicker. We don't want that. We want him to experience every bit of agony of each cut," he says. "Once you down enough, you'll be able to hold the skin as you cut."

"Okay," I say as I slowly slice down. It gives resistance as his muscles tense, but I continue until I can grab a hold of his flesh. Nash stands behind me and has his hands over top of mine, guiding me. I press too deep in one spot, causing blood to spurt out at me.

"Whoops," I giggle. I glance up and realize that my rapist has passed out. "Aw. Not fair. I didn't get to pass out."

"He will wake up soon. Just a few more cuts and we get to have a little fun," he says with humor in his tone.

I hold the skin taut as I continue carving until the skin detaches completely. It feels almost like rubber in my hand, except bloody. “It’s like pig skin,” I say. “How ironic... since he’s a pig.” I say, and Nash laughs.

I move to start a new strip and this time Nash moves his hands to my waist. I take my time. The exposed muscle glistens from the slickness of the blood. When I drop the last piece of skin, I step back to admire our work. It’s like an art piece when you consider all the blood, sweat, and tears that led me to this moment. I can’t wait to get my hands on the men who started this chaos that is my life now.

“That was fun!” I say brightly. “What’s next?”

“I’m thinking... sulphuric acid and hydrogen peroxide,” he says.

“You can just buy acid like that?” I turn to ask him.

“Yes,” he chuckles. “You can buy it in hardware stores, online, even some bigger retail grocery stores carry something similar. It’s just battery acid.”

“Damn. That’s convenient,” I say. “How many people have you killed?” As soon as I ask, I realize that’s something he may not want to divulge. Does he trust me that much?”

“Ah, if I tell you that, I’d have to kill you,” he winks. I internally flinch at that comment but shake it off.

“Isn’t that the goal here?” I ask.

“Unless I can make you beg,” he says with a playful grin.

“Mmm. Good luck,” I say dismissively.

I move over to the table and take my coveralls and gloves off while Nash goes to the storage closet in the corner of the room where the trash can is.

I can't help but wonder what my life could be like with Nash. He says that I am his, so why would he kill me? I want to believe he wouldn't. Maybe when he takes me back to the motel, we can sit and have a real conversation.

My thoughts quickly divert back to when I woke up to find him brushing his cock across my lips. I wanted him to ruthlessly fuck my throat. When he finally started to take control, I couldn't help but touch myself. It felt so empowering to be the reason for his moans. It felt amazing that he wanted me so badly that he lost control. The way he looked down at me, like he was proud of me, was amazing. I want to experience so much with him, but I can't get hurt again. I can't get my heart invested in someone just to be betrayed the way Jeff had done.

I realize now that Jeff didn't care about me. I don't think he ever did. He convinced a little girl that a grown man was in love with her. I should have been having sleep overs and talking about my crush in math class at fourteen, not getting bent over the hood of his car outside of my house after he brought me home from fucking in his apartment. My parents knew I was dating and having sex with him. They knew how old he was, but they didn't care. I was groomed and almost married my abuser.

This revelation sends me into a silent spiral. I have cried so much that I have nothing left to give. I have felt so much pain that nothing hurts anymore. I feel nothing and that's scarier than feeling everything.

"You okay?" Nash asks.

"Mhmm, just intrusive thoughts," I say. "So why are you mixing the acid with the peroxide?"

"It's called piranha solution," he says. "It vaporizes anything made of carbon and turns it into carbon dioxide. It's painful and a relatively quick death. You absolutely cannot get this on yourself, so I'll have you put on protective gear. I'll wake him up, and you can slowly pour it on his chest. You don't want it to splash anywhere."

"Okay," I smile.

Nash mixes the acid and the hydrogen peroxide into a glass beaker before putting a face shield on me as well as a glove that comes up to my shoulder. He puts everything away and wipes the table down before walking over to my rapist.

"Rise and shine, fucker," Nash says as he slaps him on the cheek. When he doesn't respond, he does it again. "There you are! Ready to have some fun?"

"Please," the man chokes out. "Please. I'm sorry."

"Too late for that," I say. "You didn't give me a choice, so you don't get a choice either."

"Ready?" Nash asks, carefully picking up the beaker.

"Yes!" I say as I nearly bounce over to him. He smiles brightly at me before gently placing the container of bubbling liquid in my gloved hand. "This would be one hell of a suicide."

"Lila," he says, narrowing his eyes at me.

"What?" I giggle. "Not like you could do anything about it if I throw it back like a shot."

"What the fuck is that?" the man says as he starts to pull at his restraints. When he flexes his chest, he screams in agony. His movement causes fresh blood to trickle down his torso, and I smile.

"Your ticket to Hell," I say simply. "I hope fucking me was worth it."

"*Wait, wait, wait!*" He screeches when I step closer to him.

"Awe, but I love the way you squeal" I say with a sickly-sweet grin. I slowly pour the piranha solution on his flayed and bloody chest, and he lets out a blood-curdling scream. I hand the beaker off to Nash and step back to admire the bubbly art displaying on his chest for me. His flesh turns a repulsive shade of black. The smell is putrid, but the sizzling combination is mesmerizing.

I step back and Nash wraps his arms around me from behind. Watching my rapist melt away while he screams makes my pussy ache. I lay my head back on his chest and take a deep breath. My heart is racing, and my breathing is quickened. I'm trying to calm myself, so he doesn't know how aroused I've become. His screams are like a fucking drug. Knowing that he is dying in front of me is the best feeling and the only thing I want is for Nash to fuck me.

"What's wrong?" Nash asks.

"Nothing," I say softly.

"No, what is it? I know it's a lot to take in, but I'm proud of you for getting yourself justice."

"Thank you," I say. Nash shifts and I feel his growing erection pressing against me. I inhale sharply and he chuckles.

"Oh, my sweet little butterfly," he says softly. "Tell me what you want."

"You. I want you," I breathe. Nash pulls me over to the table and pushes me to lay over it, so I'm rested on my elbows. He pulls my shirt up and tugs the underwear down before I hear his zipper. My rapist is making gurgling noises as Nash slowly fills me with his cock. "Oh, dear lord," I groan.

"Fuck, Butterfly," Nash growls. He slams into me, and it makes my breath catch. He is stretching me, and every barbell of his piercing is teasing my pussy perfectly as he fucks me.

"Oh, my God," I gasp. "Fuck. Harder. Please, fuck me harder." He meets my request with far more force than I expect, and I yell out as he pounds into me. I grip onto the edge of the rattling table and lay my head down as my moans and whimpers grow louder.

"You take me so well, Butterfly. Scream for me," he commands as he quickens his pace. He grabs me by the hair and pulls my head back as he pushes deeper with every stroke. I moan loudly when he slaps my ass. The burn that it leaves behind is delicious. When he does it again, I cry out from my pleasure and I'm practically vibrating as my climax builds.

"Come for me, Butterfly. Come on my cock," he says as he pulls me up with his hand wrapped around my throat. My back is arched dramatically so he is still fucking me deep and hard. Pain ripples through my belly and it feels so damn good. He kisses me as he squeezes my neck, cutting off my airway. A blinding orgasm bursts free and I groan as he pounds into me. Nash groans and bites the junction of my neck and shoulder, making my body jerk with force as he drains himself inside of me.

"Holy fuck," I pant when he lets me breathe again.

"Stay here," he says.

"Mhmm," I groan and lay my head on the table. He walks away from me for a moment and when he comes back, he cleans me. I am a bit taken aback by this because no one has done this before. "Why are you cleaning me?"

"Because aftercare is important," he says as he pulls my clothes back into position, and then turns me to face him. He has a sad look on his face but hides it by hugging me and burying his face in my neck. "I'm sorry."

"For what, Nash?" I ask.

"For earlier in the hotel room before he came to the door," he says. "You said... I shouldn't have..."

"It's okay. You didn't do anything I didn't enjoy," I say. "I know what I said but... it's different with you."

"How so?" he asks as he pulls away to look at me.

"I think knowing you will be the one to give me what I desire... I want you to have control. I've never been the type that wants to be dominated but with you... I want that and then some. I need you to destroy me in every way possible, but I want you to enjoy yourself while you do it."

"Is that permission to do as I please?" he asks.

"I mean, you're going to kill me one day, so sure," I shrug.

"Do you want a safe word?" he asks.

"No. I literally want you to kill me, Nash. I don't think there is a safe word to prevent murder," I say flatly. "I don't really care."

"You are so confident that I won't have you begging for me to spare you," he says, lifting my chin slightly so my head dips back.

"Eventually I'll just work up the courage to do it myself," I say. "I'm afraid of fucking it up and surviving."

"Do you think it's because you don't actually want to die?" he asks.

"No, Nash. Why would I want to stay in a world where boyfriends fuck your best friend of twenty fucking years? Where men rape women eight at a time and sometimes force them into positions where a woman has no choice but to comply. Oh, or maybe because I was groomed by Jeff and lost my virginity to him at fourteen years old and my parents didn't give a fuck. They knew he would fuck me so hard that I would get injured, but when I told Mom that I was in pain.... she said I should feel lucky that his dick can reach far enough to hurt me. He was twenty and I was hardly a teenager. They thought a trust fund would fix all of the neglect, but it just had him stick to me like glue," I ramble but stop abruptly. "What happens to goopy now?"

"I'm sorry?" he asks, furrowing his brows.

"Goopy," I say, pointing to my dead rapist. The solution completely ate away his chest and left behind exposed bone and black goop that was once flesh. There are also gaping holes, where I don't doubt, the solution ate away at his internal organs. The mixture coated his entire chest and abdomen, resulting in a hollow chest cavity filled with a slowly bubbling blackened film.

"That's... an interesting way to put that," he says, and I laugh. "We need to take him up to the ovens."

"Ovens?"

"This is also a crematorium, dear," he says.

"Oh shit. That's pretty smart."

"Normally, I cut them into pieces and distribute them among other planned cremations, but I have no one on the schedule, so I'll just have to run it out of schedule."

"Is that bad?" I ask.

"No, I just can't make a habit out of it," he says. "I'll load him and send him up in the elevator. You just sit here and look pretty for me." Nash lifts me and sits me on the table before turning to grab the metal gurney before putting on protective gear and grabbing a box of baking soda.

I watch as Nash covers the body in the white powder before loading him onto the gurney and into the elevator before sending it up.

"Do you do this at night because no one is here?" I ask.

"Yeah. I run the ovens at night anyway, but I have employees who work during the day," he says as he pulls me off the table and we go to the stairs.

"You never did tell me how many people you have killed," I say.

"A lot," he says simply.

"Well, a lot to me is like... one. So... what is a lot to you?"

"Probably around... I don't know. Maybe fifty or sixty," he says as we reach the top. I don't know how to respond to that, so I stay silent. I go to open the door, but it doesn't budge. "Oh, right."

"We were locked in here?" I ask when he pulls keys from his pocket and unlocks the door.

"You were," he says. "I had the key."

"That's... unsettling," I admit.

"It should only be unsettling if you are afraid that you'll be next," he says before smacking my ass. "Come on, Butterfly. We need to get you back to bed."

"You'd skin me?" I ask, smirking.

"No, I'll pick something even more fun for you," he grins. "I do have permission to do whatever I want without a safe word."

"Mhmm," I deadpan. "Let's burn this fucker. I'm tired."

It's almost four in the morning by the time we finally got back into his SUV. I am exhausted and I just want to sleep. I have my head laid back on the seat as I lazily watch the city go by. I am struggling to keep my eyes open, but I immediately sit up and look at Nash when we pass the motel.

"Where are we going?" I ask.

"To my house," he says simply.

"All of my stuff is at the motel," I say, panic rising in my chest.

"I'll have Daniel get rid of it," he says. I stare at him, waiting for a sarcastic smile or a jab, but he is dead fucking serious. "What? I told you that you belong to me now, Lila. Plus... you've seen my face now. No one gets to know both of my identities and go off on their own."

"I thought you were giving me the same trust I gave you?" I ask.

"I am," he says. "When we get home, I'll let you sleep for a while before I get started."

"Okay," I say simply, slumping back into my seat.

I am completely silent for the rest of the drive. I want to get rid of this pain so badly, but tonight I didn't think about what happened, not even once. I was truly happy for the first time in a very long time and now I'm afraid if I give up, I will miss the chance to see what could be for Nash and me. Maybe he's only interested in comforting me because he is excited for killing me? Maybe this is how he operates. He acts like the protector and even helps get me justice, but then takes me back to his house to torture me to death. I want to die, not be tortured to death. Maybe I should have asked for a safe word. I don't want to be in pain, but I already agreed and gave up my right to say no unless I beg for my life.

I go round and round in my head until I am pulled from my thoughts when my door opens. "Come on, Butterfly," he says, unbuckling my seatbelt and pulling me out. "Nervous?"

"Eh... I just don't know what to expect when I die", I say.

"You'll find out soon," he says. "I'm glad I can do this for you."

"It's your thing, so why not?" I say bitterly. He chuckles and unlocks his front door. Once we step inside, he turns and sticks the key back into the door, locking us inside.

"So you don't run off," he winks. "I'll take you to your room." He takes my hand and leads me upstairs.

His home has a warm feeling to it and that comforts me. Maybe he's not the sadist I think he is. Maybe the painful deaths are reserved for those who deserve pain. I am innocent, so I deserve a quick and painless death. But he's also lost track of how many people he's killed, so maybe he's just a fucking psycho. Aren't all serial killers though? Maybe he looks for suicidal people so he can have his way and they still get to die? Who knows? But like he said, I belong to him now.

We get to the top floor and go to a room at the end of the hallway. He unlocks the door and steps aside to wave me in. "This is where you'll be staying," he says as he pushes me into the room, then blocks the doorway so I am stuck inside. "Be a good girl, Butterfly."

I stand there in a slight state of shock as he shuts the door. When I hear him lock the door from the outside, I'm confused. I was only supposed to rest for a little bit before he came back. What is his definition of a little bit?

"Oookay," I say, turning to look at the rest of the room. There is a king-size bed underneath a large window. The bed has a blanket on it, so I guess I don't get a pillow. The window has no curtain and there are visible bars on the outside so I can't jump. I should be able to open it to get fresh air though. I step into the bathroom, and I see a small basket that is holding various products like shampoo, conditioner, body wash, a new toothbrush, toothpaste, a few washcloths, and two plush towels to the right of the basket. I look in the cabinets and they are empty. The shower curtain is clear and there's an obvious camera in the corner of the room. He can see everything I'm doing here.

I go back into the room and see more cameras in the corners of the room. He has this place surrounded so that he can see me at every angle. He likes to video his murders so he can relive them. Does that mean that there was a camera when we were fucking? I go to the closet and find it empty, but there are no cameras. It's small but it would allow me to sit and think without being watched.

Right now, I'm going to rest and hopefully he will be back by the time I wake up. I'm not even sure why all of this stuff is in here considering he said he would get started once I rested for a little bit.

I stripped down to just my oversized T-shirt and underwear before crawling into the bed. The blanket is so huge that I can bundle one side of it up to create a makeshift pillow while still being wrapped with the rest of it. It's chilly in this room, so the blanket is nice to have. I am so exhausted that I don't even have time to overthink what Nash will do to me before I fall asleep.

Chapter Eight

Nash

I CHECK THE CAMERA again and see that Lila is still asleep. She must be bored out of her mind, because she's done nothing but sleep for the last four days. When I go in to give her food, she eats like she's starving. She always ends up sick though. Every meal, she always throws up after. Mildred told me it was likely an eating disorder and she's stressed, so it's triggering her into binging.

Albeit it's not great, it's something we can address later. I need to bring her to the point of fighting for her life. She is nowhere near that yet. In the beginning, she looked terrified when she found out I was bringing her here. I thought for sure just being here would break her, the moment she got in that room, she regressed back to when I first met her. This tells me that in order for her to survive, right now she needs to be dependent on someone. Although I would love nothing more than her to be dependent on my care, she needs to be her own person. She needs to be able to stand on her own two feet to survive this world. If she is dependent on me, then it puts her into a position where she can't escape, and I don't want her to ever feel like there's no way out. That is ironic, considering I have her locked in a room right now, but once I get her to a point where I think she's ready to break, I will intentionally let her out to see if she will run. If she runs, it shows me that she is there. She wants to fight for her life, all I have to do is catch her and make her beg.

Watching her flay her rapist was so fucking amazing. That is the passion that I want to see from her daily. Seeing her smile and knowing it is genuine is heartwarming, but I want her to have those moments without having to torture and murder someone.

For so long, the only solace I felt was when I was killing someone. Until I met her, I didn't think it was possible to be happy outside of all the death that I bring onto the city. Finding and destroying every dark aura consumed my every thought. When I looked someone in the eyes and saw nothing but pitch black in their soul, it was almost erotic, knowing that I would be the one to watch them take their last breath. For the first time ever, I felt shame for what I had done when she asked me how many people I had killed. I was so afraid that she would reject me somehow by knowing the number. I'm still afraid that she won't want me, even if I do help her heal. I knew the risks of getting involved with her though. I know that she could ultimately become independent and decide to be alone. I'm doing this because it's best for her in the long run, not for me.

If I had it my way, she'd never leave my side. I would turn her into my perfect little slave, ready and willing to take me however I want her to take me. I would have her on her knees for me every evening when I came home. She would give birth and raise our children while still bending over for me every night. But the world isn't a perfect place and people are not everything you want them to be. Life is not a fairytale and no amount of breaking someone will make them into what you want. You see, I can break her to the point of being subservient to me, but I will never see the happiness that I saw in the basement of the funeral home. To me, that is the kind of perfection that I want. I don't want her to be subservient in the way of being a slave. In our everyday lives, I want the attitude, the sass, and the resistance. I want her to be so painfully independent that she fights me on every decision that pertains to her. I never want her to live her life being complacent. Even if she doesn't want me, even if she wants to be alone. Her happiness is all that matters, and I will do anything to give back what those men took from her. I will avenge her trauma and they will bleed for what they did.

I want to get to a place in my life where I'm not dependent on murder to survive. With her, I don't need to cause torment to wake up in the morning... but she will never know how dependent I have become on her . I will never put that responsibility on her shoulders because it's not her responsibility to ensure that I survive. It is slightly a double standard considering I want to be the reason she survives. I want to take on that responsibility but unlike Lila, I had people in my corner. Jimmy and Mildred never let me go without, they were more supportive than my biological parents had ever been my entire life. Jimmy didn't have to take me in as his child, but he did. He sacrificed so much for me, and I am more than willing to do that for someone else. Lila deserves to have someone in her corner. Now she has three people in her corner, ready and willing to take on the world for her.

"How is she doing?" Daniel asks.

"She appears apathetic," I say. "I see absolutely zero emotion from her. I can tell that she is annoyed that I don't talk to her when I go in, but she doesn't do anything. She just sits on the bed and stares at me as I sit her food and any supplies down."

"Can't you give her like a book or something? She's going to go insane in there," he says.

"She won't read it," Mildred says. "She is waiting on you to come back and kill her. She's not going to start something she doesn't think she can finish."

"Right, so I need to wait until she gets pissed that I haven't come back," I say. I park in front of the motel, and we all get out.

"I thought you got all of her stuff?" Daniel asks.

"So... I never explained what happened that led to me taking her to my place," I say. "To make a long story short, while I was watching her a few days ago, I caught the motel manager assaulting her. He basically put her into a position where she had no choice."

"Uh oh," Mildred says.

"Mhmm, so after she ran to her room, I followed. She didn't fight when I came into her room. She just went straight for the shower and was sobbing. I got her to stand up and talk to me. I helped her clean up before I got her dressed and laid her down. Once I was with her, she calmed down. When I was going to leave...

we heard him come to her room and put a key in the door. I pulled it open, and he ran."

"You had that creepy mask on, didn't you?" Mildred asks.

"Yeah. Lila wasn't fazed by it, but the manager was immediately scared. I chased him down and knocked him out. Once I got him in my truck, she asked to come with me. I had already expressed that he would die for what he did, but she wanted to be there to see it," I explain. "I took the mask off once we got in the truck, and she was significantly happier being able to see me. I told her I was giving her the same amount of trust that she gave me, so getting in the truck with me meant I could trust her enough to take the mask off. She asked my name once we got set up in the basement, and... then she got curious about my plan. She basically did seventy-five percent of it."

"She did? How'd she take that?" Daniel asks and I involuntarily laugh.

"Sorry," I say when he gives me a confused look. "She enjoyed it. I'd say that is the happiest I've seen her, and I think it's because she was taking back some control."

"What did you two do to him?" Mildred asks.

"Flayed his chest, then poured piranha solution on him," I say with a shrug.

"Dear God," Daniel says. "And she was okay with that?"

"More than okay, actually. She... thoroughly enjoyed his screams."

"Ew. Did you two fuck while he melted?" he asks with a frown.

"Sure did," I laugh. "Once she realized I was taking her to my house, she shut down. I think she is already doubting her demise, but she's too stubborn to admit it."

"What do you plan on doing once you do go in there?" Daniel asks.

"Exactly what I would do with anyone else, but without permanent damage," I say.

"Nash, do you really think..."

"Yes," I interrupt. "She has to believe that this is the end, or she will never break far enough to realize she wants to live. It's fucked up and admittedly insane but the moment those men realize that she never died... they will come for her."

"I'm confused as to why they would do all of that for some debt. Generally, they go after the person who owes the money," Mildred says.

"Especially considering all Jeff would have to do is ask Lila for money. She has that trust fund from her piece of shit parents," I say.

"Wait," Daniel says. "Who is the beneficiary to that trust? She's smart enough that she would've set something up so it would go to somebody if something happened."

"Oh... shit," I say.

"Think about it... they just happened to ditch her, and she just so happened to get attacked? The area that she got attacked is not known for activity. I've talked to most of the transients that camp in that area and no one has noticed gang activity or made any mention of a group of men hanging out. If someone was going to do something like that, they would stick to somewhere they felt comfortable," Mildred says.

"So, I need to find out if he is the beneficiary," I say. "I knew he was a piece of shit, but I didn't think he would go that far."

"This is a lot if her boyfriend of eight years tried to have her killed," Daniel says.

"It means I need to make damn sure Jessika isn't involved in plotting her murder, because she's pregnant," I say. "I'm a lot of things, but I'm not that. I won't kill her when that baby had nothing to do with it."

"I met Jessika at the hospital," Mildred says. "She's a bitch for fucking Jeff, but she was genuinely worried about her. She asked the doctor every question she could think of. She legitimately was worried about her well-being after being attacked and I don't think she knew it was going to happen. Jeff didn't step in there once while I was there, and he never asked the doctors anything."

"I need to take a deeper look into this before I bring it up to her," I say. "But this changes a lot because he could send anyone after her if he's trying to get his hands on that money."

"Why are we here?" Daniel asks.

"I bought the motel," I say. "I need to get access to the security footage so I can get rid of any evidence of her being here, her assault, and the footage of me running him down in the parking lot. I checked his phone to make sure he didn't have an app or anything and I saw the system in there when I bought it yesterday. It's a very old system, so I just need to pull the tapes and destroy them."

"And long term?" he asks.

"I'd like to turn it into somewhere that I can help people get off the streets. I don't think it's too much to ask for them to be clean and sober, so there will be a process to get a room, but I want to add accommodations for them to be able to cook, and for those who have children and pets. It can be a system where they have six months to a year to get on their feet before they get transitioned out. I was looking into other transitional housing that they could move to if needed, but the goal would be to provide services to help them get jobs and a permanent home."

"And you want me to run it, I hope," Mildred says.

"Yes," I laugh. "I trust your judgment and you are around these people every day. This would allow you to continue to help the homeless, but also make it to where you are not living paycheck to paycheck since you don't want to take money from me."

“I’d love to help,” she smiles. “I’ll need a few people to help me since this place has almost a hundred units.”

“That will be fine. I have many investors who have reached out between yesterday and today to help fund it. It’s easy to get people to donate to things like this because it’s a tax write off. It makes them look good, but also allows me to help more people. Obviously, there are some people that I won’t take money from,” I say. “I already have everything I need plus some for renovations. I’ve already recuperated the amount that it took to buy this place.”

“That’s wonderful,” Mildred smiles. “I think this will be really good for many reasons.”

“Let’s go get rid of all this shit,” I say, glancing at my phone. “She’s awake... and pissed.”

Chapter Nine

Lila

I OPEN MY EYES and I'm annoyed that I am waking up to an empty room again. I am so sick and fucking tired of being in this goddamn room. He doesn't say a single word to me when he comes in. He hardly looks at me. He told me that I would rest for a little bit and then we would get started, but we haven't started shit. Is this how he's going to kill me? Is he just going to bore me to death until I just hang myself? That's not a bad idea. Maybe he will get jealous and want to kill me himself.

I get up and go to the bathroom to pee before going back to lay in bed. All I do is stare at the fucking ceiling. I regret giving him full control considering he isn't fucking doing anything. I am growing angrier by the minute. I get off the bed and start to pace, counting my steps as I go. I am trying to calm down, but I can't. I am on the brink of losing my fucking mind.

I go to the door and try to open it, again. When it doesn't open, I kick the wood with the sole of my foot. I do it again and again until I am out of breath. I start pacing again, trying to pull myself back into reality. I'm trying to chill out because I do not want to be this mad when he walks in. I keep walking from end to end for what seems like an eternity.

When I hear a key slip into the lock, I turn and get to the door before it opens. As soon as we make eye contact and he smirks, all of my rage slips out.

"*What the fuck is wrong with you*?" I yell at him and shove him away when he steps closer to me. "What fucking happened to letting me rest then getting started?"

"Have you not been resting?" he asks calmly as he steps into the room and shuts the door.

"No, I've been losing my goddamn mind in here," I scream at him.

"Who cares? You are just going to die in the end anyhow, so what does it matter if you are a little bored?" he says.

"I care, you *fucking* psycho," I scream and push him again.

"Damn, where was all that fight when you were getting raped?" he asks.

"*Fuck* you," I seethe as I slap him across the face. I recoil immediately when I realize that I just hit a serial killer. I question why that's a bad thing, but I'm distracted when he laughs.

"We would have had a problem if I had actually felt that," he taunts me.

"You're a fucking asshole,' I snap. "You can't just fucking lock me in a fucking room and disappear."

"I can do whatever I want," he says as he steps closer. "I *own* you, remember?"

"No one owns me, prick," I say with venom in my tone. "It wouldn't be very nice of me to start when you are so wound up, so I'll come back later," he says with a grin. He walks toward the door.

"Just fucking kill me already, goddamn it!" I scream and shove him from behind. His reaction is so fast that I gasp when he spins around and grabs me by the throat before shoving me against the wall. I can't breathe suddenly when I realize that my feet aren't touching the ground.

"I will do what I want, when I want. Keep being a little brat and you won't be able to sit without the memory of me fucking your tight little ass flashing through your mind," he growls. The look on his face is feral in a way that pisses me off. I stay silent for long enough that he sets me back on my feet and I cough and gasp when he lets go of my throat.

I'll admit… that makes me want to be a brat more so he will fuck me. I also want to prove that I want to die and if he won't do it, I will. He turns abruptly and leaves the room, locking the door behind him. I am still standing where he left me, but I am thinking.

I have thought of so many ways to kill myself, but this room is so bare. It takes me a second to figure it out but when I do, I can't help but grin as I go over to the bed and throw the blanket to the floor before pulling the sheet off.

I start tearing the thin material into strips before braiding them into a rope. It's thin enough to manage but strong enough to hold my weight. Once I'm done, I tie it into a noose and stand on the bed to attach it to the top of the canopy. My goal is to be able to just step off the end of the bed and that should do the job.

I go up on my tiptoes and secure the rope before slipping it over my head. I laugh when I hear Nash stomping toward me. When I step to the edge of the bed, his pace quickens, and I laugh. Turns out he really does want to be in control. Maybe I'll get lucky, and it will just snap my neck.

As soon as the door starts to open, I step off the bed without a second thought. Nash screams something at me and my brain floods with thoughts when the noose tightens around my throat. My body instantly rejects what I have done but I can't think. I don't even get a chance to know if that's what I wanted or not before Nash lifts me up and yanks the rope off me.

"Aw. He cares," I choke out between coughs before he growls and throws me on the bed. Without a word, he starts ripping my clothing off until I am naked.

"What are you doing?" I yelp when he picks me up and tosses me over his shoulder. "Put me down, damn it!"

I start hitting his back, trying to get him to put me down but he just swats my ass over and over until I stop. Tears well up in my eyes from the burn in my ass caused by the force of his hand. He carries me through the house and down to the basement without a word.

He sits me on my feet, and I see that there is a leather lined table in the center of the room with restraints. There is a table filled with various things from a paddle to knives. When I see the same jugs of ingredients needed for the piranha solution next to a heating plate and beaker I start to panic.

"Oh, it's far too late for that, Butterfly," Nash says. He bands his arm around my waist and pulls me closer when I try to back away.

"Nash," I say hurriedly. A wave of fear comes over me and the screams of my rapist play in my head on a loop as he forces me onto the table and restrains me face down. My legs are spread wide, and my arms are pulled straight out to my sides.

This is what I wanted.

I wanted to die.

I gave him permission.

I want to die.

He wants to torture someone.

I wanted this.

I gave him permission.

Goddamn it. This is what I wanted.

No safe word. Just pain and death.

Nash lifts me and puts a bolster under my hips so that my ass is up, and I am exposed to him. I force myself to look away from that bottle of acid and breathe. My body is trembling but as long as I'm not looking at it, I can calm down some.

"I get to decide when you take your last breath," Nash says with anger in his voice as he pulls something over my head. Everything instantly goes dark. He fastens what feels like a collar around my neck and the covering tightens as more straps wrap around my head. There is an opening at my mouth. He pushes what feels like a dildo into my mouth before attaching it to the covering. The dildo reaches back far, but not so far that it makes me gag. *Did this fucker just put a gimp mask on me?*

"Look at *my* butterfly," he coos. "Spread open and waiting for me like the needy whore she is."

I flinch when he runs his hand up my inner thigh but stops short of touching my pussy. He slaps my ass and I gasp as I pull at my restraints. The sting is intense and when he does it again in the same spot, I cry out as my pussy clenches. He pauses between each smack and the pain gets more and more intense. When he finally stops, my ass is burning but I am whimpering from how it makes me ache to be fucked. I moan when he pushes his fingers into me.

"Your cunt is fucking dripping for me, Butterfly. Do you like the way I spank your perfect little ass?"

"Mmm," I moan. He starts to roughly fuck me with his hand making me nearly scream from the intense pleasure it creates. He abruptly pulls out and I groan when I feel empty.

When he smacks my ass again, I scream from the shock of the paddle burning my ass more than his hand did. He hits my ass repeatedly even though tears are spilling out of my eyes. I still want him inside me so badly. I love every second of the pain that he is causing.

He stops and starts fucking me with his hand again and my thighs shake as he brings me to the edge of an orgasm. I whine when he stops but that quickly turns into a pained scream when he strikes me with what feels like a flogger. Each hit is in a new spot, and I growl and groan as he no doubt covers me in welts from how hard he is hitting me. When he stops, my entire body is trembling, and it feels like my back is covered in raw nerve endings.

My breath catches and I try to pull away when sudden shocks shoot throughout my back in little pin pricks. It feels like an electrified pinwheel is being rolled over my back. After a moment, I get used to it and moans slip out of me when he dips it between my legs to run it over my lips. My legs are shaking when he spreads my pussy and gently runs the pinwheel over my clit. My moans become desperate, and I involuntarily rock my hips.

Nash stops abruptly and I hear him toss everything down before he takes the dildo out of my mouth and takes the entire head covering off. He then moves to get on the table behind me.

"Oh fuck!" I scream out when he sudden grabs my hips and slams into my pussy. He grips my waist and starts to fuck me so hard that I am screaming as tears roll down my cheeks. This might be a punishment fuck but it's the most amazing feeling to be used by him in a way that gives him complete control over me. Orgasms pour out of me, one by one until eventually he groans and pushes deep to flood me with his cum.

When he moves away from me, I hear him messing around with something. I hear him sit something close to me before I feel him push a massive dildo into my pussy. I hear a bottle cap open proceeded by him slowly pushing another dildo into my ass. It starts to move in perfect rhythm where one is pushing in as the other pulls out. I then hear the vibrations before a wand is pressed against my clit and I cry out as intense pleasure throws me into an orgasm.

"Be a good girl while I'm gone." he says as he turns on what I have now realized is a fucking machine pounding into me. I open my mouth to object when the dildos move faster and push deeper as the wand continues to vibrate against my clit.

"Fuck, you can't just leave me here," I groan as my body tenses, and I cry out as an orgasm is forced out of me again. I whine when I hear the door shut. This is going to be a long fucking night.

Chapter Ten

Nash

I GO UPSTAIRS AND sit on my couch to watch Lila on the camera. It's a bit evil for me to leave her down there attached to all of that, but I think overstimulating her is a good place to start before I set in on scaring the hell out of her.

I am not excited about this because I simply do not want to hurt her emotionally or physically, and it could cost me her all together if she doesn't understand why I am doing this. I need her to survive though, even if it's without me.

When I saw her step off that bed and immediately start thrashing, I felt like I had failed her. I didn't expect her to escalate like that, so I am still concerned that she is past the point of being able to want to live. I know I won't be able to kill her, no matter what I've promised. I would then just have to put her into a facility where she could be treated long term and remain safe. That's honestly where she should be now, but I'd rather just do this than risk someone coming after her again and no one be there to protect her.

When she saw I had the acid and peroxide out, she started to panic. As cruel as it is, I'm going to use that fear to my advantage to scare her. When I go back down to the basement, I'll start with methods to fuck with her.

Watching her on the camera isn't as fun as seeing it in person. Her entire body is tense, and she is moaning loudly as the machine fucks her tight little holes. I have the wand turned up, so I am certain she's overwhelmed at this point. She has squirted twice already, and I can't help but stare in awe at how well she is taking this.

Trying to get her to face her trauma is inadvertently making me face my own. I know why I do the things I do, and I wish I could stop. I'm terrified that Lila will reject me and I will go right back to killing. It is fucking suffocating to have those thoughts all the time. I suppose I could get mental health help, but at this point it'll only land me in jail. I need to find a way to help myself. It's not fair for me to put any of this on her. She has enough going on, but in the same way it might help put some things into perspective, not being a serial killer is something to write about.

Up until Jimmy adopted me at 16, I lived my life recklessly like Lila did. I have no regard for my life because no one could hurt me the way my mother did; the way she allowed me to be used by others. I'm convinced she was on drugs when she had me. I can only remember a handful of times that she was sober for more than a few hours until she would have her drug dealer come and rape me as payment. She traded me for drugs so often, I don't know how I never caught anything from some of those nasty and vile men having their way with me.

That's not even including her weekly fucks who would beat me or touch me. They were worse because they would catch me when I was sleeping. I spent a lot of time under my bed hiding, because it was the one place she could never find me. I think the only reason I had my own room was so there would be a private place for people to take me as payment for her drugs. She had plenty of money because I was her currency. How fucked up is that? You grow and birth a child just to repeatedly allow people to hurt them. After the men left, she would always try to act like a parent, but she would be too high. If I had known then how to make her overdose, I would've done it in a heartbeat.

It was risky to set the house on fire, but she was so fucking high that she couldn't stand up. I found way too much joy in that moment, seeing the look on her face when she knew she was going to die. If I could go back, the only thing I would have done differently was I would have found a way to hurt her the way she hurt me. I don't think there's any way to create that kind of pain.

Everyone wants justice for their trauma, but no amount of revenge is going to take that pain away. No matter how many I see and destroy, it will never change the fact that my mother let men rape me repeatedly so she could get high. It doesn't change that she would lock me in my room for days at a time, while she had men over to fuck for cash.

I was really fucking lucky to end up with Jimmy when I was placed in foster care. He was the only other person, besides Mildred, that I talked about killing Mom with. He shared my excitement when it was listed as an accidental death due to a candle getting knocked over. He even taught me how to use the ovens, so I knew what to do when the funeral home was mine. He knew I would kill people who were bad. It was hard to explain to him that I just knew that they were bad, but he trusted me. I would tell him who I wanted to go after and he would always look them up to make sure I was right, and I was. I go after everyone from pedophiles to rapists to predators in general. I will happily go after any drug dealer who cuts their shit with fentanyl. I will go after the parent who sells their child for drug money. I will go after anyone who causes an innocent person harm. I don't care how much money they have or their social status.

I think the kill that I am most proud of would have to be the police chief. There was a rumor going around he was raping his daughter. It took me a while to get in contact with the daughter, but I was able to talk to her with my mask on and tell her basically what I wanted to do. I just needed to confirm the rumors that he was hurting her. She realized that he was more than just depraved. The police chief was fucking demonic. He had been raping her for as long as she could remember, and she was forced to have two abortions due to him getting her pregnant. She pulled up her shirt slightly so I could see her abdomen, and she was covered in bruises. He thought that it was possible she was pregnant, so he kicked the fuck out of her and broke her ribs. What he didn't realize was super early in gestation the baby is pretty well protected, so he had no idea where to effectively kick. She said that she had plans to run away, but she was afraid that he would still find her. I told her that I wanted to get rid of him for her and her only request was that she wanted to watch him die. From there, she was able to lure him to the funeral home under the guise of her having to identify her friends' body, and she was nervous to go alone. Once he was inside and it was just me, I think that's the point he knew that I would be the one to end his life. He willingly walked back there when I told him to lay down in the cardboard box on the table. He wasn't wearing any of his work gear, so he had no way to fight back. He tried to apologize to his daughter, and the only thing she said was she was going to raise her child, knowing how they were born, but teaching them to do better in life. I simply opened the door and shoved him in before closing it. We sat and listened to his screams, but they didn't last long. That oven can get as hot as 2000°, so it wasn't long before the screams went silent. About two or three hours later, we swept out his remains and disposed of him in a dumpster. The city went crazy when she reported him missing. She played the role of grieving daughter perfectly. I still check in with her from time to time. It was a miracle her daughter was born without any severe complications from being a product of incest.

The worst day of my life was when Jimmy died. There in the end he was rapidly declining in health. I had hired the best nurses and doctors I could find to care for him when he was diagnosed with stage four pancreatic cancer. He told me that I was wasting my money when I could just end his life for him. Of all the people in the world, he was not one of the people I would be able to kill. Lila is now within that category; I can't kill her. I would love her though. He would happily avenge her trauma with me.

When I decide that I've sat here long enough, I stand up and walk back to the basement. This is it. This is where I have to convince her with fear that she wants to live. I pray to God that it works. I don't want to live in a world where someone so kind can't find their way back to the surface. Watching her drown in her trauma is awful. I won't be able to survive this if she doesn't. If she still ends up taking her life after this, I know the guilt will eat me alive and I will end up killing myself just to be with her again.

Chapter Eleven

Lila

My brain cannot decide if I like this or not. I have never come so many times in a row, but this would be the best way to die. I would be a liar if I said that I was hoping this isn't how Nash plans to kill me. I am so overstimulated; I can't think straight. My belly hurts from the way the orgasms tense my body, but each time one of the waves surges through me, it's like Heaven on Earth.

Anytime I'm able to form thoughts I always imagine that it's Nash fucking me, and that always result in me squirting. The way he fucked me through every bit of his anger was unlike anything I have experienced, and I hope to God he does it again before he kills me.

I hear the basement door open before his footsteps grow closer. I expect the machine to get shut off, but instead he comes around to the head of the table. This is probably the second-best scenario. He fists my hair and yanks my head up before gripping the base of his cock that he has already pulled out.

"Open up, Butterfly," he says with a smooth tone. I open my mouth and extend my tongue slightly, so his piercings don't catch on my teeth. He immediately pushes to the back of my throat and holds my head in place as he fucks my mouth. He is unrelenting as he thrusts through my gagging but stops for a second every once in a while, so I don't throw up. I moan and whimper as he brutalizes my throat. When I'm not actively coming, I suck him as hard as I can, hollowing my cheeks. His moans are delicious, and I feel proud of myself for being able to take him like this. Will he miss the way I give him free use of my body? Will he miss me at all when I'm gone?

"Mmm, fuck, Lila," he growls as he fucks my throat. "That's it, Butterfly, take it all like a good girl." He groans as his thrusts become shorter and more staggered as his cock pulses, his come coating my tongue and the back of my throat as I eagerly drink him down.

When he pulls out, he lets me rest my head and goes around to shut the machine off. Once he has removed the dildos and machine away, he removes the bolster before unhooking my restraints. I don't fight him as he rolls me to my back. He secures the restraints again but this time my ankles are together and extended out, and my wrists are restrained together and straight up above my head. I focus on taking long deep breaths. Every time he walks near that table, anxiety swells in me.

He gets something out that looks like a box with knobs to turn and wire leads coming out of it. "What the fuck is that?" I ask, and he chuckles.

"Transcutaneous electrical nerve stimulator," he says. "It's a TENS unit."

"You're going to electrocute me?"

"I sure am," he says nonchalantly as he sticks pads to me. He places them underneath my arms, the bend of my hips, my sides on my rib cage, and between my legs on my inner thighs. He then attaches the leads to the pads.

"That's a hell of a way to kill someone," I sigh and close my eyes.

"Oh, this won't kill you," he says. "It will hurt though."

"So, you're just going to torture me to death? You should've just let me fucking hang," I spit at him.

"Oh, but it's no fun that way," he says.

"Fucking psycho," I mutter.

"Lila... look at me, please," he says. I sigh heavily and open my eyes.

"What?" I growl.

"Are you sure you want this? Once I start this... I'm not entirely sure I can get myself to stop," he says.

"What happened to stopping if I begged you?" I ask, frowning.

"I never said I could actually stop, I just said that's the only way I would," he says. "Do you want this?" I hesitate before I eventually nod. "You don't seem very sure."

"I want this," I say. I don't think I'm strong enough to move on from this.

"Alright," he shrugs. Nash walks over to the box and starts adjusting the knobs before plugging all of the leads in. He comes back over to me and lifts my hips to put a towel under me. I grow more confused when he pulls it into place as though it's a diaper.

"What are you doing?" I ask.

"I am a lot of things, Butterfly, but I'm not going to do something knowing the result and not do anything to help," he says.

"Wha..." When I go to ask him what he means, he flips the switch on the box and pain surges through my body. I scream and my body arches off the table involuntarily. He pushes me back down to the table before adding a strap to keep me in place. When I get myself to stop screaming, I groan through gritted teeth. When it stops, I relax into the table, but my body is shaking.

Nash adds another lead to the TENS unit and places a small probe against my clit. "Fuck," I whine.

"Again?" Nash asks.

"You're an asshole," I choke out.

"Oh, but I sure do know how to make your cunt ache for me," he says humorously. I go to say something, but he turns the TENS machine back on and I scream. I realize immediately what the towel is for when warmth rushes out of me no matter how hard I try to stop it. I should feel embarrassed about pissing on myself. At first, I think he did it intentionally but when a blindingly painful orgasm hits me like a punch to the gut, I understand the goal is simply to overstimulate me.

"You know, Lila, it's a shame that you never changed your beneficiary to your trust," he says simply. "He wanted you dead before, so I guess he will still get what he wants."

The realization sweeps over me and I feel like a fucking idiot. It was in front of me the entire time, and I didn't know it. He's been the beneficiary since I was eighteen and anytime we mentioned marriage he would get mad because I always brought up a prenup. What better way to get all my money then to have someone fucking kill me? The only problem is, they didn't anticipate anyone finding me.

"Fuck," I groan. I'm so angry suddenly but I can't do anything about it if Nash kills me. I can't protect my money if I'm dead. He will pretend like he's the broken boyfriend while I am nothing more than a pile of ash. I suppose if they don't find a body then he won't get the money if they can't prove I'm dead. Do I really want to take the risk that he will take all my money for him and that skank that used to be my best friend?

"What is it?" Nash asks.

"Stop with the... the shocking," I force out.

"Okay," he says as he flips the switch, and all the painful sensations go away. I'm a little taken back when he starts removing the leads.

Once he has everything put away, he goes to the table and picks up a knife. Not any knife. The same kind of knife we used on my rapist. "Fuck, fuck, fuck," I hiss. Panic starts to boil over when he walks to the other end of the table and grabs the beaker.

"It's convenient that the solution is so easy to make," he says.

"Nash," I say.

"Yes, Butterfly?" he asks as he continues to mess with the bottles and the heating plate with his back to me.

"I didn't do anything wrong. Can't you just strangle me or something?" I ask.

"Nah. I like this method. Plus, you'll be dead soon anyway. What does it matter?" he asks as he turns to me with a beaker full of clear liquid. It looks exactly the same as what I dumped on my rapist, but it also looks like water. He sets it down next to me before picking up the knife.

"Do you not care about me at all? Would you really want me to suffer?" I ask, trying to reason with him.

"I thought I was a psycho, Lila?" he says. "This is what psychos do."

He digs the blade into my chest and cuts down my sternum. It's not deep, but it's enough to make me groan. I'm nearly panting when he picks up that beaker. The closer he gets to me with it the more I start to panic.

"Nash. Don't. Please don't make me like this," I plead.

"You'll be dead soon you won't be mad at me for long," he chuckles. I squeeze my eyes shut and think about everything that led me to this moment.

"Stop, stop, stop. Please don't," I yell out.

"Too late, Butterfly," he says with a smile as he tips the glass container. I involuntarily scream before it ever even touches me but then all the adrenaline pumping through my veins comes to screeching halt when nothing happens. "You have to clean cuts, or they'll get infected."

It was just peroxide.

And now he's just fucking with my head.

"I think I have a better idea, so you don't have to see me doing it," he says as he unhooks my restraints.

When he turns back to the table, I realize that I'm free. He assumes I won't run. I watch him for a moment, thinking about what to do. I could stay and risk him not having the self-control to stop or I can run and get the fuck off this property. I don't care that I'm naked.

When I see him grab the container that I know has the acid in it, I instantly realize that I don't want to die. I don't think I ever wanted to die. Was the rape so fucking devastating that I'm okay with being vaporized by some solution cooked up in a basement? In this moment, I start doubting every single time I told myself that I wanted to die. When faced with that beaker, I think I just didn't want to have to face everything that happened. No matter how much I tried to ignore it, I couldn't. I was so desperate to not have to feel it that I tried to numb the pain every way I could think of. Somehow, that led me to suicide. Somehow suicide seemed more desirable than facing the trauma. It's terrifying to think that I will have to live with this forever, but it's more terrifying to think of him pouring acid on me.

I swing my legs off the table and jump down. When he spins around, I immediately turn and run. I race up the stairs and through the kitchen until I find the front door. When I throw it open, I waste no time running toward the woods. I know the road is gated, but surely these woods lead out of here. I can always try to hide out for a while and make him think that I got off the property.

"You can't hide from me, Butterfly," he calls out.

I have no idea what to do or where to go, but I need to make sure that he doesn't kill me. Maybe if I just stay away from him for a long enough, he will be able to pull himself out of this. I know he has got to have a traumatic past to be brought to something like this. I want to believe that he's a good person. I definitely think that I have fallen for him.

I want to be the reason that he doesn't feel the compulsion to kill anymore. Even if that means that he has to be dependent on my emotional support, whatever he needs me to be. I enjoyed being spanked and flogged by him so if that's what he needs, I will willingly give myself over to him for that.

I feel like I owe him my life, even though I pressured him into the situation that I don't think he ever wanted to be in. He has shown every bit of hesitance and has tried to talk me out of this, but I wouldn't budge until it was too late for him. I can't get mad at him for something he warned me about. I don't know what he screamed at me when he walked into that room when I stepped off the bed, but I could hear the pain in his voice. He was scared. He never wanted to be the one to hurt me and I think everything was to see if I would change my mind.

My body is weak but I'm not in pain. In the moment it was so intense but now it just feels like my muscles have been overworked. I am sore from him railing me as hard as he did, but that's a given. I just want to curl up with him and sleep, but I would like to actually wake up.

I am running through the woods, and I think I'm alone until suddenly I'm not. Nash wraps his arm around my waist and slings me to the ground before straddling my body with my hands pinned above my head. His facial expression is so much calmer now, but it doesn't stop me from panicking when I see he has a knife on his belt.

"I'm stabbing you one way or another. It can be my cock or my knife... your choice, Butterfly."

"Don't. Please don't. Please, Nash," I beg as tears roll down my cheeks.

"Say it, Lila. Tell me what you want," he says softly.

"You, Nash. I want you. I don't want to die. Please don't hurt me," I say through near sobs.

When he lets go of my wrists and kisses me, I immediately grab his face. Everything about him relaxes, so I do too. I can feel all of the trauma that I packed away, cracking open to reveal raw feelings of that night all over again. I know it is going to hurt to heal, but I will do anything to keep having moments like this with him. Moments where we are both vulnerable but connected.

"I'm sorry," I say through tears. "I know you didn't want to do any of that."

"Shh, baby. Don't apologize," he says. "I hated every second of it. I swear to God, I will make up for everything I did."

"Please fuck me," I sniff.

"Are you..."

"I'm sure. Please. Everything you did was things that I asked for. You didn't cross any lines, Nash," I say, cupping his cheek. "But I want you to fuck me like you hate me. Please. I want it hard and mean."

"You are amazing," he says before he kisses me softly. "From the moment I heard you screaming, I knew I wanted to be the one to make you sound like that."

"Please," I whisper.

"Anything for my butterfly," he says, with a devious smile as he sits up and pulls his cock out.

"Fuck, you're huge," I say, wiping away my tears.

"Mmm, but you take me so well," he says as he leans down and kisses me. "Do you trust me?"

"With my life," I breathe.

"Safe word?" he asked.

"Uhh." I replied.

"Fight me, Butterfly" he whispers in my ear. I grin when he pulls back to look at me. I place my hands on his chest and try to push him back so I can pull my legs out from under him. He swiftly grabs my wrists and pins them, so I start to wiggle and thrash under him to try and free myself. I can't help but giggle at how he looks at me and grunts or growls when I try to pull my hands away. I get an idea suddenly and I freeze.

"Wait, wait, wait," I say, faking a surge of anxiety. Nash instantly let's go of my fists and sits back when he hears the panic in my voice.

I am quickly able to turn my body enough to where I can try to crawl away and run. I'm not quick enough because Nash immediately grabs my hips and pulls me back, making me squeal and giggle. "You little brat," he laughs and puts a hand between my shoulder blades to push my chest to the ground.

"Oooooh fuuuck," I groan as he slowly fills me with his cock.

"You're mine, Lila," he growls as he slams into me, making me cry out. "We will get you revenge for what they did. We will heal together."

He fucks me harder with each passing word. My insides feel like mush as he holds onto my hips and ruts into me. It's almost primal the way he takes me. His growls are delicious, and my mind is numb with pure bliss.

"God, I'm gonna come. Please, make me come. Oh God, Nash. Oh God," I nearly scream. It feels as though he is trying to wreck my insides and I want everything he has to offer. I want it forever.

"Oh, my pretty little whore," he groans. "Take my come, Butterfly... such a good girl."

I push my hips back to push him further into me. Every time our bodies meet, we both moan. We quicken our pace until I am screaming as ecstasy pours out of me with each stroke. He harmonizes perfectly with me as we both fall into our orgasm, desperately moaning.

"Fuck, you're amazing," I groan when he pulls out of me.

"So are you, Butterfly," he says as he kisses my back and gets up. Before I can get up, he manages to fix his pants, then scoops me up into his arms. "What are you doing?"

"Taking you home," he says. "I'm going to give you a bath, massage lotion into your skin, feed you, then we will go to sleep," he says.

"I think I have an eating disorder," I mumble as I snuggle against his chest.

"I know," he says. "Everything is going to be okay though."

"How do you know?"

"Because you are the strongest person I know. If anyone can overcome their trauma, it's you," he says. "I will be here through everything. No matter what it is, I will never leave your side."

"I'm going to give you an ultimatum. I don't like being this person, but I think it's important," I say cautiously.

"Let's hear it," he says as he carries me.

"After we get revenge, no more killing. No more torture, unless it's torturing me with forced orgasms," I say.

"Honestly, I would be content not going after them for revenge, but the fact that they were likely paid by Jeff to kill you..."

"They'll want to finish the job," I sigh.

"Exactly. The moment they realize, they'll come after you. Leaving Jeff definitely saved your life," he says. "Enough of that for tonight. No one can get on this property, so we need to focus on you."

When we get back to the house, Nash takes me to the master bedroom and sits me on the bed while he draws me a bath. I am exhausted by the time he gets me into the tub. I groan when he lowers me into the hot water. The water smells like chamomile and vanilla. It's soothing and luxurious.

Nash takes his time washing every inch of my body. I still have some welts on my back but he is extra careful to not irritate them. When he's done, he gets me out of the water, dries me off, and lays me on the bed. I am lying on my belly, and it doesn't take long for me to fall asleep with him rubbing lotion into my back.

Chapter Twelve

Nash

I AM PROPPED UP on my elbow, looking down at Lila. She is gorgeous all of the time, but there is something about how peaceful she looks that is so damn special. She fell asleep shortly after me putting lotion on her back. I finished what I was doing, then dressed her and now we are here. I am watching her sleep, and I am so thankful she has the wherewithal to understand that I was desperate to try and get her to see that she wants to heal. I could see on her face that she didn't want to die but she was hurting so badly that she felt she had no other choice.

I slowly get up from the bed, doing my best not to disturb her. I can't help but gently brush the hair from her face before leaning down and kissing her forehead.

I feel my phone buzzing in my pocket. When I pull it out I see it's the camera at the front gate. Daniel and Mildred are here. I know they are about her, so I figured they'd show up .

I let them in the gate before I change clothes and go downstairs to meet them. As soon as I step off the stairs, the front door opens.

"Hey," I say as I sit on the couch.

"Lila asleep?" Mildred asks.

"She is," I nod. "She's been out for about an hour."

"So? How did things go?" Daniel asks as they sit across from me.

"Well... she broke," I say vaguely.

"How?" he asks, and I sigh. "Obviously she's alive and hasn't run away from you, so..."

"I made her believe I was going to use the acid," I say. "Also... when I got home, she was angry. I left the room to let her chill out and... she made a noose..."

"Oh my God," Mildred says. "Did she..."

"Yeah," I say. "I walked in right as she stepped off the bed. She has bruising, but it's not terrible. I got to her pretty quickly."

"Oh my God," Daniel says.

"Yeah, I think she knew I was watching her and could get to her. She made a comment saying I cared about her... I think that's the only reason she did it."

"Yeah, if she was confident enough that you would save her, I can see that," Mildred says. "What happened next?"

"Just a lot of overstimulation," I say. "I used a TENS machine because it's the only thing I was comfortable with that I knew wouldn't cause damage."

"Ow," Daniel says. "Then?"

"Then I cut her chest a little and poured peroxide on it. I thought for sure it would break her, but it didn't, so I took the restraints off and turned my back to her. The second I touched that bottle of acid... she bolted," I explain. "I chased her down and the second I got to her she broke."

"You fucked her in the woods... didn't you?" Daniel asks.

"Yeah," I say with a smirk. "She... we are on the same page with a lot of things... she did give me an ultimatum though."

"Oh?" Mildred asks.

"Mhmm. She said after getting revenge... No more killing or torture," I say.

"How do you feel about that?" she asks. "Does she know about your trauma?"

"She doesn't know specifics yet, but I'm okay with it. If I want her to heal then it's only fair that I do the same."

"Think you can manage?" she asks.

"I do," I say. "Outside of the fucker who raped her, I haven't really wanted to. It used to consume my free time but now... I just think about her and all the things I want to do with her. I want to give her the life she deserves."

"And she knows that Jeff probably set this up?" Daniel asks.

"Yeah. I'll have my lawyer help her get Jeff removed from her will. She will have to think of a replacement or set up a donation maybe," I say.

"You've not been in a serious relationship in a while," Mildred says.

"Yeah, I know. She and I both have a lot to learn," I say.

"That you do," she nods. "Both of you are incredibly strong. It's okay to lean on each other for support. Asking for help doesn't mean you're dependent."

"Yeah," I sigh. "I just hope I can help her heal."

Chapter Thirteen

Lila

One week later

IMMENSE PRESSURE SLOWLY DRAGS me from my dreams. I realize that my legs are up at the same time as I feel the pressure deep in my belly again. Waking up after taking sleeping medication is hard and it takes a second for everything to come into focus.

"Nash," I groan.

"Shh, let me use this sweet cunt, Butterfly," he says softly as he slowly fucks me.

"Fuck that feels good," I pant, as he starts to quicken the rhythm of his hips.

Nash has his arms hooked behind my knees but when he leans into me, he folds me in half as he thrusts deeper into my pussy. He wraps his hand around my throat then starts fucking me harder. His pace is growing relentlessly and all I can manage are whimpers when he bottoms out.

"You look so pretty when you can't breathe, Butterfly." He slams into me, making my back arch before saying, "Such a gorgeous shade of blue." Nash leans down and softly kisses my lips while railing into me so hard that it makes my insides ache. He loosens his grip on my throat, and I hear my phone start to ring as I suck in a breath. Nash immediately slows.

"Answer it," he says with a mischievous grin.

"Nash," I whine.

"Answer the phone, Lila," he orders. I reach over and grab my phone with a heavy sigh.

My eyes go wide, and I shake my head when I see that it's my dad. "I can't..."

"Answer it, Lila," he repeats. He sits back and brings my legs to his shoulders as he fucks me slow and deep.

"H-Hello?" I answer, trying not to moan. Nash puts my phone on speaker before laying it on my chest between my tits.

"Hello, Lila," my father says. "Did I wake you?"

"No, you didn't. What's up?"

"Haven't talked to you in a while. How are you?" he says. I sigh, knowing Jeff called them.

"Considering you only call me when Jeff calls you to bitch about me, I'm assuming you already know how I am," I say simply. Nash starts slowly rubbing my clit and my entire body relaxes and he smiles at me.

"I wish you had called us, Lila," Dad says.

"What do you want, Dad?" I ask.

"We are in town. Meet us at Ruby Château at noon," he says.

"Is that a question or a demand?" I ask as I bite back a moan as my legs start shaking.

"Please meet us, Lila," dad says. "We haven't seen you in months."

"That's because you two decided to move to England," I say. "You only call when you want something from me, so what do you want now?"

"We just need to talk to you is all. Will you be there?" he asks.

"Fine, but I'll have my boyfriend with me," I say and Nash gently pinches my clit, making my eyes roll back.

"Boyfriend? You just left Jeff," dad says with a disapproving tone.

"I think I'm entitled to do whatever I want, considering Jeff and Jessika were fucking for two years," I say, nearly groaning aloud.

"What's his name?" Dad asks.

"Nash Sutton," I say. I cover my mouth and hold my breath when he starts fucking me harder again. He is still pinching my clit hard, and I am shaking as my orgasm threatens to burst out of me.

"He owns Papillon Security Management," Dad says. "Isn't that where you work?"

"Yes," I choke out. "I'll be there at noon."

"Alright," he sighs. "Please dress appropriately. This place..."

"I got lunch there every day for months. I know," I say. "I'm gonna go."

"Okay. Love you..." he starts to say but I end the call and toss it away from me.

"Please make me come," I plead. He grins at me before flipping me to my belly and pulling me up to my knees.

"Stay," he says as he gets off the bed. I stay where I am, wondering what he has planned. I hear him open a drawer somewhere in the room, then he gets back on the bed behind me. "Do you trust me?"

'With my life," I say confidently.

"Good," he says. I flinch when I hear the pop of a cap. "Do you understand what I'm going to do?"

"Yes," I whisper.

"Take this," he says as he nudges me with something. When I grab it, I see that it is a Rose Toy. It sucks your soul out through your clit. He tied me to the bed a few days ago and made me come until I was in tears, then fucked me so hard that I nearly blacked out. I sense it's about to happen again.

"You're going to give me brain damage one day," I sigh.

"Highest setting and don't move it. If you do, you'll be punished, understand?"

"Yes," I say as I turn it on. It comes to life, and I reach between my legs to put it to my clit. I moan loudly and Nash spreads lube on my ass.

He wastes no time slowly filling my ass with his cock. We both groan as he pushes deep. I am on the edge of coming. The pain being twice as much pleasure, and I just want him to fuck me until I can't see straight.

"Harder," I whine. "Please, harder."

Nash responds to my pleas by tightening his hold on me, finding an unrelenting pace as he tries to destroy my insides. I scream out as he forces an orgasm from me, but he doesn't let up. He keeps pounding into me until eventually I end up lying flat on my belly with the toy wedged between me and the bed. It is still sucking away at my clit, but my arms are pinned under me.

"Fuck, Butterfly," he growls, slamming into me so hard that tears sting my eyes, but I'm still moaning desperately as orgasms flood out of me one by one. I can't form words or thoughts. I scream into the bed as my whole body convulses under his. I feel so free being used as his personal fuck toy. None of the pain can sneak in when he is balls-deep inside of me. Anytime I am overwhelmed, one or both of us coming clears my mind.

Nash ends up with his forearms to either side of me and he kisses and bites my neck as he groans and fucks me harder and deeper. When he starts moaning and whimpering as his orgasm approaches, it fucks with my head. Something huge is building inside of me and I feel as though I'm going to erupt.

"Oh... fuck... yes... God... Yes," I moan.

"Come with me, Lila," he says before biting down on my neck. I explode like a volcano and when all the pressure releases, I come hard and my arousal floods out of me and soaks the bed beneath our bodies. Nash groans and growls as he pushes deep and fills me with his come.

He brings himself down on top of me, but that toy is still sucking me hard. I am completely pinned and moaning loudly. Nash laughs and wraps his arms around my body before burying his face in my neck. I feel cocooned as I writhe under him. His cock is still buried in my ass and every time I clench my muscles, he groans. Over time, I feel him grow inside of me. He groans as he starts to fuck me again. His thrusts are punishing, and it only makes me scream louder.

"Come for me," he growls. We both fall together this time and, once again, my arousal floods out of me.

"Please stop," I whine. "I can't take anymore."

Nash pulls out of me and pulls me up to get the toy. I grumble when he makes me get up. My body feels heavy, but I drenched the bed so I can't lay there. He moves me to the couch under the big bay window before getting what he needs to come back and clean me up.

"That was amazing," I mumble. "I want to sleep now."

"Sleep, Butterfly," he says as he pulls the blanket off the back and covers me up. "I will clean up and wake you when it's time to get ready."

"Thank you, Nash," I smile at him.

"You're welcome, my love," he says as he leans down and softly kisses me.

Chapter Fourteen

Nash

We pull up to the restaurant and Lila sighs as she lays her head back on the seat. I put my hand up to tell the valet to wait. "You okay?" I ask.

"I just really hate being around my parents," she says.

"We can go," I suggest.

"No. They'll leave me alone for a while after this. I only talk to them every few months," she says. "Let's get this over with before I change my mind."

I nod and get out before walking around to her door. I hand the valet a hundred-dollar bill for holding up his line before opening the door for Lila. When she gets out, I wrap my arm around her waist to keep her pulled close to me.

"Breathe, baby," I say quietly. She nods but is quickly slipping into a detached state. She walks along with me, but I can see on her face that she wants to run.

Over the past week, we've talked about everything. I told her all the gritty details about my childhood, and she told me what happened step by step in her rape. It's easy for her to identify her parents neglect but beyond that, she is unintentionally evasive when anything deeper about her relationship with her parents or Jeff comes up.

My theory is that she endured physical abuse from her parents and possibly Jeff. George R.R. Martin once wrote "people learn to love their chains," and that could not be any more accurate. Sometimes the abuse you endure becomes all you know, and you find solace in normalcy. Breaking away from that, even if it's to a safer environment, means changing everything you've ever known. Everyone has their limit though. Lila's was cheating with Jessika.

When we get into the restaurant, I pull her aside. "Just say the word and we are gone," I tell her.

"Okay," she says quietly. She is holding onto my arm tightly and I can feel her body trembling.

"You're not alone, Butterfly," I tell her. "I won't let them hurt you physically or emotionally. I won't abandon you."

"You promise?" she says as she looks up at me. Tears are brimming at the surface, and I know she is hardly holding on.

"I promise," I answer with a soft smile as I gently stroke her cheek. "I'll always be here."

"Let's do this," she says with more confidence. We turn and walk to the host stand. Lila grabs hold of my hand and stands as close as she can.

"Name under the reservation?" she asks kindly.

"Monroe," Lila says. "Two should be here already."

"Yes, ma'am. Follow me," she says kindly.

Lila is still trembling, but she straightens her back and walks with confidence. She's used to putting on a mask for everyone, just like me. We allow ourselves to be vulnerable with one another because the other knows the evil that lurks behind feigned smiles and kind words. It's in this moment that I realize I am more than just falling for her. I'm in love with my Butterfly.

We get to the table and a woman who looks exactly like Lila, only older, stands and rushes us. "Hey, Mom," she says with a sigh.

"Lila. How are you? Are you okay?"

"I'm okay, Mom," Lila says. "Can we sit? People are staring."

"Yes, yes. Sit, please," she says. The man stands and hugs Lila and it's hard to not miss how she tenses at his touch. He lets his hands rest on her lower back and she immediately pulls away and returns to my side.

I pulled a chair out for her on the opposite side of the table from her parents. Once she sits down, I take the chair beside her.

"I am Audrey, and he is Phillip," her mother says. "And you are Nash, yes?"

"Yes, ma'am," I say simply.

"It's a pleasure to meet you, Nash," she smiles. Phillip is giving me an eat-shit-and-die look, which just adds to my theory that Lila was sexually abused by her father. That makes me wonder why he was okay with Jeff grooming her at fourteen. Unless he is the one who set them up when she was a child... or he sold his daughter off to a pedophile in exchange for security of the future of his company. Jeff's family is wealthy and well-known on Wall Street for their stock exchange deals.

"Likewise," I say kindly. I lay my hand on Lila's leg and gently stroke her inner thigh. She instantly melts at my touch.

"What happened?" Phillip asks Lila.

"Dad," she sighs.

"Jeff told us the basics, that you were raped when you were out at a bar alone," Audrey says.

"Yeah, because they ditched me to go back to the apartment and fuck. Did he mention that he had his dick down her throat when I called to ask where they were because I couldn't find them?"

"Watch your mouth, young lady," Phillip growls. Lila immediately shuts down and shrinks in her seat slightly, leaning into me.

"So?" Audrey asks.

"So… I was walking home to try and catch them," she says. "A group of eight men grabbed me and dragged me into an abandoned flower shop. They left me tied up with a concussion until a woman found me. I was at the hospital for twelve fucking hours while they did an exam and give me fluids because I was pretty dehydrated. I went back to the apartment and slept for a while. When I woke up, I found them having sex in the living room. I just packed my stuff and went to a motel."

"You have all that money, and you went to a motel?" Dad asks.

"Yes. Truthfully… I contemplated suicide and even tried once, so I didn't care where I was staying or what happened to me," she says. "Nash saved me from myself."

"So, you're with him because your boss didn't let you kill yourself?" Phillip asks.

"I didn't know he was my boss for about a week. He wasn't aware either. I work under someone else, and I don't get to his side of the building often."

"Are you still working?" Audrey asks.

"Not at the moment. I need to fully process this before…"

"Hey guys. Sorry we are late," I hear a man say behind me. Lila stiffens, but I can see rage on her face.

"You've got to be fucking kidding me," she says with a grave tone.

"Lila, be respectful," Phillip scolds.

"Hell no!" she says. I can't help but smirk at her when she suddenly gets a backbone and stands up for herself.

"Don't be a child," Jeff says as he takes a seat with who I presume is Jessika. She is meek and keeps her head slightly bowed.

"No." Lila says with dry laughter. "I thought you were into children, or was that just me?"

Jeff frowns deeply at her before turning to Phillip. "How was your flight?" he asks.

"It was nice. Thank you for asking." He has an air of conceit about his tone that makes me internally roll my eyes.

"Who are you?" Jeff asks me.

"My boyfriend," Lila says.

"Really? It's been what... three weeks and you are already fucking someone else?" Jeff asks and Lila laughs, making him frown again.

"You were fucking my best friend for two years, Jeff. You don't get a say so over what I do with my body. Not after what you did," she says with the same icy undertone that she had the night we murdered the motel manager. She is full of rage. Jeff's eyes widen as the realization comes over him that she knows he tried to have her killed. He is speechless, so I take the time to push this conversation along so Lila will feel comfortable letting some of that rage out.

"Well... what he had eight other men do," I say.

"What?" Audrey says to me. "What are you talking about?"

"Jeff... what is she talking about?" Phillip demands. Jessika looks up and glances at me before looking at Lila.

"Lila... what do you mean?" Jessika asks. She flinches when Jeff moves, but she is entirely focused on Lila.

"Oh, you didn't know? Your little boyfriend paid those men to kill me for all of the money he was supposed to get if I died," Lila says. "He didn't anticipate that they would gang rape me and leave me for dead. The men who raped me didn't expect someone to find me. Luckily for me... I changed my will a few days ago."

"Who did you change it to?" Phillip asks. I'm not sure why that is important right now, considering she just told them she was nearly murdered.

"Nash," she says.

"What?" I ask, confused. "I thought you put Mildred?"

"No, I know she wouldn't want all that. You have enough money of your own that you won't try and murder me for mine," she says before turning to Jeff. He is seething but when he speaks, he is calm.

"You are mistaken," he says coolly. "I loved you."

"Did you love me when you'd rape me until I bled at fourteen?" she snaps. "How about when you'd slap me repeatedly, so the marks wouldn't show? Did you love me when you fucked my best friend?"

"You need to stop. Now," he says, his anger slipping into his tone.

"Or what? Are you going to hold me down and fuck me, hoping I will beg you to stop, the way I did for the last eight years? You know, I was convinced that it was normal and okay for you to do that just because we were dating. Also, because my darling mother told me that I should feel lucky that you wanted me at all?"

"Lower your voice," Phillip growls.

"Fuck you!" she says as she abruptly stands. Her chair falls back and hits the hard tiled floor, grabbing the attention of everyone in the restaurant. "Fuck all of you. You sexually assaulted your daughter only to sell me off to some fucking pedophile, so you could hand your goddamn company off without everyone abandoning ship when you brought a stranger in."

"Sit down, Lila. You are causing a scene," Audrey says with a hushed tone.

"Absolutely not. I am done being a doormat for everyone to use and walk all over like I mean nothing," Lila yells. "Nash showed me what it means to have bodily autonomy. You three are vile and wicked. I hope you all burn in Hell for how you've hurt me. I hope you lose everything the way I did, but I pray no one helps you pick up the tattered remains of your life the way Nash has done for me."

I stand up when Phillip does. "Let's go home," I say as I lean down and kiss her head. Her body relaxes before she turns and kisses me softly.

"Okay," she says as she smiles. She seems almost relieved, as if a mass amount of weight has lifted off her shoulders. She's learning to navigate this world without being controlled, and she is doing wonderfully.

"Don't you walk away from me," Jeff says as he stands.

"Fuck you, Jeff," she says simply before turning to Jessika.

"Did he really have those men hurt you like that?" Jessika asks.

"Yes," Lila says. "Jeff is a dumbass and forgot I'm a computer engineer. Not only did I find the entire conversation and transaction where he paid them one hundred thousand dollars, but I found the texts where Jeff mentioned their plan to keep control over me so he could have the family business going to shit. This lunch was to ask me if I will show up to a meeting and give my blessing to the board for me to forgo getting the company when Dad dies."

"I didn't know," Jessika says tearfully. "I swear to God, I didn't know. I... Jeff, we are done. I let all of this go on for far too long. I didn't even want to ditch her that night. I wanted to be with my friend and tell her what was going on but.... I'm going to go."

"I know," Lila says. "You're still a cunt for fucking my boyfriend, but he has a way of convincing people of anything. Just... get away from him, before he tries to have you killed too."

"Sit," Jeff growls when she goes to stand. Jessika stands anyway.

"He was trying to convince me to get a will and list him as the beneficiary," Jessika says.

"I hope you didn't do it, or you should expect to get gang raped soon," Lila says with a shrug.

"No, I haven't done it," she says. "Can I walk out with you two?"

"We can drive you," I say.

"Yeah. I don't trust someone won't be waiting for you down the block," Lila says.

"Thanks," she says.

"You'll regret this," Jeff says with a threatening tone.

"Awe. Are your wittle feelings hurt, Jeffy-poo?" Lila says with a baby voice before poking her bottom lip out. Jessika and I laugh at the same time, making Lila giggle.

"Come on, ladies," I say. "We can get some lunch after Jessika gets her things."

"Oh. Can we go to that little diner with the dollar sliders?" Lila asks, nearly bouncing. Jeff rolls his eyes at her excitement but I just chuckle.

"Anything for you, Butterfly," I say, taking her hand in mine and kissing it. We turn and start walking toward the front. I can't help but notice that Jessika flinches again when Jeff reaches for her.

The girls are silent all the way out of the door before we are stopped. Lila yells and is suddenly pulled away when Jeff grabs her arm and yanks her toward him. Rage sweeps over me and I instantly turn and grab him by the throat slamming him back against the brick pillar.

"If you ever put your hands on my woman again, I'll break the fucking things off," I say with a grave tone. "Don't look at her, don't think about her, and if I have to repeat myself… I'll fucking kill you. Have I made myself clear?"

"Yes," Jeff chokes out.

"Good," I say as I let go of him and step back to wrap my arm around Lila's waist. She giggles and takes my hand. Fuck, I love how giddy she is when I want to make someone bleed for her. I will make the rivers run red with the blood of anyone who dares hurt my butterfly.

Chapter Fifteen

Lila

I AM SO MADLY in love with Nash. It hit me all at once when he had Jeff pinned against the brick. Jessika looks fucking terrified, and I suspect it's because she went against Jeff. I know what I endured when no one was around, so I imagine she went through something similar.

I still think she's a skank, but at this point, I think she's likely traumatized as well. "You good?" I ask as I grab her arm, pulling her along with us.

"Uh...yeah," she says. "Thank you for this. Really," she says as we get to the SUV. Nash tips the valet and we all get in.

"You really didn't know?" I ask her.

"No. I didn't even want to... he never gave me a choice," she says quietly.

"You mean he raped you?" I ask.

"I didn't say no."

"If you didn't want to, that was rape. Considering he's raped me for years; I think I'm qualified enough to make the assumption that he forced you. How did it start?"

"Two years ago, I got really drunk," she says. "You were out of town and... I don't even remember how it happened. One minute I was in my room drinking alone, and the next he was on top of me. Everything was so fuzzy... I don't even remember having all that much. You know I don't drink excessively to the point that I black out... He told me that I came onto him, and I pushed him until he caved. Then, he would make me have sex with him or do things to him so he wouldn't tell you that I forced myself on him."

"Jessika," Nash sighs. "He drugged you."

"He did that to me once when I threatened to leave him for fucking one of his employees. He drugged me and I woke up to him on top of me," I say. "And he just kept doing that?"

"Basically. I got stuck in a loop of not wanting you to know how long it had been going on. I didn't know a way out without telling you, but I guess I should have. I just... he was so goddamn convincing that I'd lose you and he would make sure I never spoke to you again. A few times he threatened to kill me but... I don't know. I wish I had told you. If I had maybe you wouldn't have been hurt by those men."

"I probably still would have. I didn't even think about my will until Nash asked me," I say.

"You seem happy," she remarks.

"I am. Nash is everything I've ever wanted," I say. "He saved me from myself and has taught me how to stand up for myself."

"I'm glad you got away from them. Especially your dad," she says.

"Yeah, you've never liked them," I say.

"No, because they let a grown man rape you," she says. "I remember holding your hand while you nearly sobbed from the pain after he assaulted you the first time."

"Yeah, that was bad," I say. "It took so long to heal the tearing because he kept doing it over and over. Eventually, I started my period for the first time, and he avoided me like the plague. I was able to heal before he started up again."

"Did I hear correctly that your father molested you?" Nash asks.

"Yeah," I sigh. "Lots of touching and making me touch. There was oral a few times and some penetration a few times after I was older. It stopped when I started dating Jeff, but he still gets handsy every now and again."

Nash grips the steering wheel until his knuckles turn white. He grits his teeth and it makes a vein bulge from his temple.

"Hey," I say softly, laying my hand on his leg. "If it counts for anything, I'm done with them. They can't touch my trust but even then, I don't care. I'm done being abused by everyone."

"How could someone do that to their child?" he asks. "I could never imagine doing that to someone, let alone my child."

"You want kids?" I ask with a grin. "I'd love to practice." Nash smiles but chuckles when Jessika giggles.

"You're silly," he says, grabbing my hand and kissing me. "I'd like to have children, but it's not the end of the world if I don't."

"I want kids," I say. "I want two."

"Yeah?" Jessika asks.

"Yeah. I never wanted kids before, but I do with Nash. I think he would be an amazing dad," I say.

"You two look good together," Jessika says. "I'm really sorry, Lila. I never meant to hurt you."

"I know," I say. "I just need some time to process this. I understand it was assault and I'm not trying to minimalize that, but I just need time to trust you again."

"I understand. I'll do anything to get your trust back, so I'll be patient," she says. "I'm going to go to Dad's, I think."

"Yeah. Your dad will fuck Jeff up. Best if you just hang out there for a while. Work remotely and just stay low for a while."

"What about you?" she asks.

"He can't get on the property and I'm going to work from home for a while, so I don't really go anywhere right now without Nash," I say.

"How old is he?" she asks.

"Thirty-five. He's my new daddy now," I say. Nash and Jessika laugh heartily, and I smile. "He doesn't know this yet but... I'm in love with him. I've never been happier."

Nash squeezes my hand before kissing my knuckles. "I love you too, Butterfly."

Once we drop Jessika off at her dad's, we start to make our way back home. We have a little bit of a drive, so I decide to thank Nash for all he's done today by giving him head.

I unhook my seatbelt and he glances over and smirks as I move closer to him. "What are you doing?" he asks.

"Thanking you," I say, unhooking his belt. "What better way to say thank you than to suck your dick."

"Fuck, you're so sexy when you're horny," he says as I pull his cock free and lick my lips.

"Don't wreck, it'd be a shame to kill me now" I say as I bring myself down to lick up the backside of his cock. He groans deeply when I start sucking on the head.

"Oh, dear God," he moans when I gently squeeze his balls, fisting my hair. I instantly take him down my throat and start sucking hard while still squeezing and massaging his balls. I feel the truck come to a stop as he shifts into park. My movements become frenzied when he leans his seat back. Nash's moans are simply perfect as he lets me have control. Each time he gets close to coming though, I back off and edge him. He wants to come, but I don't let him. I love how he sounds when he is desperate for release.

I can feel his cock pulsing in my mouth, but I stop for long enough that he loses the orgasm. He growls and pulls me off of him. "Panties off," he says as he puts himself away and gets out of the truck. I laugh when he comes around and pulls me out so he can bend me over the seat. I gasp when he jerks my underwear down, but he gives me no warning before he surges into my dripping wet pussy.

"Fuck," I yell.

"This is what happens when you edge me," he growls and slams into me again. I yell each time he bottoms out and his pace quickens to a punishing speed. His aggressiveness pulls an orgasm out of me in record time, and it only fuels him further.

"Fuck... Oh... God... Yes... Oh, yes," I moan loudly between thrusts. "Nash... Harder... Please, harder."

"Come with me, Butterfly," he moans. He pulls me up enough that he can pinch my clit hard, making me scream and my body shake. He covers my mouth and I brace myself as he punish fucks me. My orgasm rips through me and I nearly scream as it continues to move through me slowly. He is moaning as he aggressively chases down his release.

He growls as he pushes deep and drains himself inside me. "Fuck, I love you so much, Butterfly," he mumbles.

"I love you too, Nash. So much," I say breathlessly.

Chapter Sixteen

Nash

Two weeks later

WE'VE BEEN PLANNING ALL week on how to get a hold of these eight men, but it's ultimately come down to using Lila as bait. We have Daniel and a few trusted men who do vigilante work like I do. Mildred has gotten nearly thirty members of the homeless community to help, including the ninth man who assaulted her. We found out that although he did assault her, he really is not of sound mind enough to understand that what he did is wrong. He understood that someone had hurt her, but he knew he wasn't causing her pain, so he assumed it was okay. It doesn't excuse what he did, but Mildred has found him a group home that will take him in so he can get the care that he needs.

Lila was insistent that nothing bad could happen to him because he saved her. He took advantage of her, but he made sure he wasn't hurting her and got her help. I can understand why she is committed to protecting him.

I am nervous that they will get a chance to hurt her again, but she is confident in us and our ability to keep her safe. Allison is going to be out there as well and is equally as confident in us.

Lila is surprised that Allison likes her so much after she gave Daniel head. She only recently found out that I knew about their encounter, but I reassured her that what she did before me is none of my business. Daniel and I have talked to Allison and asked her how she would feel about Daniel having sex with Lila. We all know they are enamored with each other. We are all in agreement there can be a separation between lust and love. I also desire to watch, then join in. Once Daniel finishes, I'll hold her down and fuck her the way I know she likes to take it. I have no problem sharing because I will absolutely wreck her when it's just her and I lying together. I will remind her that I am the one who fucks her the best and make sure she understands who she belongs to.

Daniel is laser-focused on her and he is eating it up. Her demeanor will flip the moment we bring it up though. She is terrified of upsetting me. At first, I thought she was scared of me, and it hurt a bit because I was worried that I actually did traumatize her.

Jessika was over to hang out with Lila and she explained to her that Jeff was mentally abusive to her. He would yell at her and belittle her for the simplest of things. Suddenly her behavior made sense. She is overly apologetic for things that aren't her fault. I thought it was just who she was but it's trauma. She is so used to things being her fault that she takes on all the blame. I snapped at her once when I had a migraine, but immediately apologized. She looked so surprised that I apologized and was quiet for a while. I thought it was because she was upset at me, but she explained that she didn't know how to respond. Now I know it's because she was waiting for me to actually be mad.

"Before we meet everyone, I need to talk to you," I say to her. Daniel grins and Allison chuckles.

"Is everything okay? Did I do something?" she asks.

"No, Butterfly," I say with a smile. "I just have a question."

"Okay," she says cautiously as she sits forward with her elbows in her knees. "What's up?"

Daniel is sitting next to her, and her eyes nearly roll back when he runs his hand up her back and drags his nails down. He continues to do this, and she relaxes completely. Allison looks absolutely feral watching her husband with another woman.

"Are you attracted to Daniel?" I ask simply. Her eyes instantly go wide, and her breathing quickens as fear sweeps over her.

"Uhm... uh... I don't know," she stammers.

"Butterfly, it's not a trick question. I want to know before I ask my next question. Daniel adores you, and I know you are aware of that," I say, and she nods. "So?"

"Nash, I... I am with you. I promise..."

"Stop," I say, and she sighs. "I know this fear is coming from what Jeff has done to you. I know it's worse now because you are still processing everything but understand that I know the answer, and I support it, but I just want to have a conversation. So... are you attracted to Daniel?"

"Y-Yes," she says quietly. She sighs and closes her eyes when Daniel moves his hand under her shirt to continue to rub her back.

"How do you feel about having sex with Daniel?" Allison asks. Lila snaps her head to her with a look of shock in her face.

"W-what?"

"Everyone here wants to see Daniel fuck you," she says. "It's obviously up to you but understand that Nash and I want and support this. Nash will most definitely help and do more to you after. We all recognize that there is more to sex than being in love with someone, and we know you trust Daniel, right?"

"Yeah... I do," she says quietly. She won't look at Daniel, so he gently lifts her chin so that she is looking at him.

"What's on your mind?" he asks, and she shakes her head. "I don't want you to answer right now. I just want to know if you are okay?"

"I'm okay," she says in a small voice.

"Good. What's on your mind?" he asks.

"I… isn't that cheating?" she asks.

"Cheating is deception, sweetie. Jeff lied to you and hid what he was doing. Nash will be there and will be very much enjoying the situation," he says, stroking his thumb across her cheek. It's amazing to see how she melts for him like she does for me. "You are in charge. You say your safe word, everything stops. I don't care what is happening, I will stop. Okay?"

"Okay," she says softly.

"Just think about it and we can address it after we handle everyone," Daniel says.

"I want to hurt them," she says. "I don't want you to see me differently."

"Not gonna lie," I say. "It was hot as fuck to see her with that motel manager."

"I bet so," Daniel says with a smirk. "I'm looking forward to seeing her in action."

"Oh, me too," I chuckle. "She's incredible."

"I'm just excited to see both of you fuck her," Allison says.

"How are you okay with him sleeping with others?" Lila asks Allison.

"Because I know he will always come back to me," she says. "He is and always will be in love with me, but I recognize that he can lust for another."

"Aren't you afraid someone might try and steal him away or something?" she asks. "Not that I would but I…"

"Baby, if someone can steal him from me… they can have him. If he would be willing to set aside everything we have for another woman, we were never meant to last anyway. I am secure enough in my relationship with him that I know he will be in bed with me at night. I am the one he will grow old with. So, if he wants to fuck you to tears every now and then, I'll happily watch."

"That's hot," Daniel says, and I chuckle.

"And you are okay with this?" she asks me.

"There are very few people that I trust, but Daniel is one of them," I say. "If you want this, then I'd love to watch before I help him fuck you."

"Both?" she asks with wide eyes.

"Yes," I say. "I promise, it will not be like anything you've experienced before."

"It won't hurt?" she asks with a small voice.

"It will be a bit uncomfortable for a moment," Allison says. "But they will take good care of you."

"I... I just don't want to lose you," Lila says to me.

"I'm not going anywhere," I say with a smile. "I will talk to you if I have an issue. Okay?"

"Okay," she smiles.

"Answer when you're confident and comfortable," I say. Before I can continue talking, she stops me.

"I'll do it," she says. "I'm okay with it."

"I need you to be very specific about what you are allowing," Daniel says.

"I'm okay with having sex with you," she says.

"Are you saying yes because you want to or because you think that's what we want?" I ask.

"Both. I want this, but I'm not confident in myself. You three wanting this also gives me confidence," she explains.

"Okay," I say. "Then understand that he has my permission to do whatever he wants with you if you want it also, as long I know what happens."

"What do you mean? What would happen?" she asks. Daniel smirks at me before grabbing her face and kissing her. She relaxes in his hold immediately, so Daniel pulls her into his lap. I watch as he grinds her hips against his and she moans softly. Allison is grinning but looks feral all at the same time. He presses his thumbs into the bend of her hips, and she moans louder.

When I realize he's going to make her come, I instantly get hard. Something about the way Daniel looks at her makes me want to fuck her more. I'm excited to introduce her to this side of things. Sex is how she copes and processes her trauma, so I want to give her more outlets for that.

Allison is about to implode but when Daniel slips his hand down the front of Lila's shorts, she gives into the temptation and slips her hand down her own shorts as she sits back in her seat. I get up and move to sit on the couch with them. I want to see the look on her face whenever he makes her come. I want to see if it's the same way she looks with me. She is so completely lost in his touch that she doesn't notice that I'm closer. Daniel looks over and gives a nod over to Allison, who is almost lost in her own touch as she watches her husband finger fuck another woman.

Chapter Seventeen

Lila

I AM IN DANIEL'S lap, he has his fingers deep inside of me as he makes a "come here" motion. He is hitting a spot inside of me that has my eyes rolled back and I'm shaking as he whispers to me. I hear other moans on one side of me and I know is right next to me. Allison is getting herself off while Nash is watching us closely.

"I can't wait to fuck this tight little pussy," Daniel whispers softly in my ear. "Come for us, Lila. Let me hear you."

My head is jerked back, and I gasp right as Nash kisses me hard. Daniel takes the opportunity to push deeper and suddenly he hits my G-spot more directly and I moan loudly as I rock my hood against his hand. His palm rubs against my clit this way, so I move faster.

"Look at you, Butterfly. You like the way he touches you?" Nash asks.

"Yes," I moan. I go to close my eyes, but he wraps his hand around my throat.

"Eyes on me while he makes you come," Nash demands.

"God, I'm so close," I moan. Daniel abruptly stops but stays inside of me. "No," I whine.

"Be a good girl and suck his cock," Daniel demands.

"Please," I say to Nash. He wastes no time pulling his cock out and fists my hair again.

"Open up, Butterfly. Give me your throat." I do as I'm told without hesitation, and Daniel starts moving his fingers inside of me again. I gasp and Nash pushes his cock to the back of my throat. I am squeezing Daniel's biceps to keep myself from pushing someone away. I don't want this to stop, but my anxiety decides things for me that I don't want. I refuse to let me get in my own way.

Daniel is keeping my orgasm at bay, but my body feels like it is covered in raw nerve endings. "Fuck," Nash moans when I suck harder. He's close.

"Come for us, Lila," Daniel encourages. He hits something just the right way and I start to come undone. "There ya go. That's it."

Nash groans and pushes deeper when his orgasm takes over. As he comes, I drink him down as my own climax crests. As soon as he is pulling out of my mouth, Daniel pulls his fingers out of me and brings them to my lips. "Clean up the mess you made, pretty girl."

I suck gently on his fingers and the sweetness of my arousal floods my tastebuds. I keep eye contact with him as I clean his fingers and he looks at me like he is seconds away from destroying me.

"We should meet the others before Daniel attacks her," Allison laughs.

"She's right," he smiles deviously. "Ready for revenge, Lila?"

"Mhmm," I say happily.

"Have a plan?" Nash asks me as he lifts me out of Daniel's lap to set me on my feet. My legs are shaky, which makes Nash and Daniel chuckle.

"I do," I say. "I'm going to make them hurt the way they hurt me."

I am wearing a short strapless dress. It shows off my tits perfectly and it hardly holds my rounded ass. My fishnets and five-inch heels pair perfectly with the rest of the outfit. I look sexy as fuck, and I feel good about myself again. My long, platinum-blonde hair falls in beautiful curls down my back. The contrast between my bright hair and sun-kissed skin is like a work of art. It sways in the wind as I walk down this familiar sidewalk on this beautiful mid-summer night.

I haven't been here since the night I was attacked. It's weird, but not frightening. That night I felt invincible. I followed simple rules, like crossing the street, but I never should have been here. I should have waited for a cab. I see the world a different way now and I am fully aware of my surroundings. I know what evil lurks in the shadows. I see the stares from greedy men as I walk confidently. I see the men and women of the homeless community watching me. Their instructions were clear; if I get into trouble, help. I pass by an alleyway, and I smile when I see Daniel and Nash. They respond with a smile and a wink as I carry on.

I see the group of men and I take a deep breath. This is it. This is how I will get my revenge. They think I am just a dumb blonde with a death wish, but they don't know the monster they created. They think they're invincible; they don't know the evil that lurks in the shadows. Don't they know I was never broken? I'm stronger now. They will never hurt me the way they did before. When they take their final breath, it is my face they will see as they fade away. I will do as they did to me, but I will finish the job. I will win.

"Back for more, Lila?" A familiar man asks. I haven't seen him yet, so I keep walking.

"Just trying to go home," I say simply. I see him out of my peripheral vision just as he is approaching. Stan Fields is thirty-two. He is a high school dropout and has no family. He grew up in foster care after his parents died, which is unfortunate, but it doesn't excuse his actions. Just four weeks ago he was the monster from my nightmares, but now he's dead, he just doesn't know it yet.

"No, I think you're here to play. Couldn't find a man to fuck you the way I can?" Stan asks with a smile as he steps in front of me.

"I'm pretty sure I can find someone to do more than half-ass flaccid humping," I say with dry laughter. "You could dry up Niagara Falls with that chode."

"You dumb little bitch," he growls as he wraps his hand around my throat and pulls me so that I am nose to nose with him.

"What's wrong, Stan? Can't get hard unless they fight you, huh?"

"Take her inside," he says as he shoves me toward another man. Carl Richards is a twenty-eight-year-old man, who has an ex-wife with a restraining order against him for beating her nearly to death. I'm about to do the world a favor and get rid of yet another pest. He was one of the three that assaulted me at one time.

"Awe. It's Carl. How's the wife, Carl?" I ask. He slaps me across the face, and I smile as he pulls me into the abandoned flower shop. "Better without you, I'm sure."

"How do you know our names?" Stan asks as he gets in my face.

"Because I'm a computer engineer, idiot," I laugh. "I know your name, your parent's names, your siblings, every job you've ever had, your driver's license number, your social security number, I know what medicine you take, I know everything, Stan. Sorry about your dead family."

"I'm going to fucking kill you, Lila," he growls. All eight men surround me, but I keep eye contact with him. I will not back down. His hand comes up, grabs my top, and jerks it down, making my breasts spill out. I don't react and it makes more rage surface in his eyes.

I see movement behind Stan, and I smile again as the others react by backing away from me. "Wrong move, Stan. Don't you know Wraith is looking for you?"

"Oh fuc..." he goes to say, but one blow to the back of his head makes his body collapse to the dirt covered floor. Daniel has on a mask identical to the one Nash wears, but I know which man is mine. Nash steps closer and his hands come up and cup my breasts before gently pinching my nipples, making me giggle.

"Shit. She's with Wraith," a man named Colton says. He is one of the men who joined Carl and Edgar in raping me after Stan. He fucked my throat while I cried. I'm going to have fun hurting these men.

The place is swarmed by members of the homeless community, as well as a few people who have my best interests at heart. One of these is Roy, the man who found me. Nash was worried about me being around him and in a way, so was I. I know what he did is wrong, but he isn't capable of understanding that. He never meant to cause me harm. Yesterday I talked to him for the first time, and he was so happy to see me. He asked how I was doing and asked how Nash was treating me. It took time for Nash to warm up to him, but when he playfully smacked my ass and Roy shoved him away from me, he instantly liked him. I assured Roy that Nash wasn't hurting me, and I was okay with him doing that. Roy hugged Nash and apologized for hurting him, which breaks my heart because there is no reason he should be on the street to fend for himself. Luckily, he has Mildred to make sure he doesn't starve to death. I'm not sure he would be capable of caring for himself on that level.

"Look, man, we were only doing what Stan told us to do," Edgar says. Edgar is the one who raped me while Colton assaulted my throat. He is also the one who pissed in my mouth and made me throw up. I didn't find much about his history other than that he is thirty-five and has always been in trouble. He has charges for everything from first-degree rape to larceny to possession of narcotics.

"That's the fucker who pissed on me," I say with a controlled tone.

"Hmm. Interesting," Nash says as he walks closer to him. "Tell me, Butterfly... what else did he do?"

"He raped me vaginally while Jerome raped me anally," I say, pointing to the man beside him. Jerome is twenty-seven years old and still lives with his meth-head of a mother. "Brad and Tony raped me together at the end of everything."

"Who is the one who made you throw up during the rape?" Daniel asks.

"Stan," I say. "Jerome did the thing with the dog shit. I think it was Colton that hit me in the head."

"Alright. Let's get them to the funeral home," Nash says. A few people step up and hit my rapists just as Nash hit Stan and they all hit the floor.

"You ready for this?" Nash asks as he takes my hand and leads me outside. The incapacitated men are restrained at their ankles with their hands behind their backs. Their arms and legs are then tied together and brought out to the SUV, where they are carelessly thrown into the back.

"Yes," I say happily. "You know... the mask is kinda hot. Before I was okay with it because I thought you would kill me, but you should definitely chase me down with that on one day."

"Mmm. That sounds like a wonderful idea," Nash says as he playfully smacks my ass. "Ride with Daniel and Allison. I don't want you in the truck if they wake up and someone gets loose."

"No," I say, shaking my head. "At least Daniel needs to be with you."

"Oh?" he asks humorously.

"Yes," I say firmly. "And don't pull the macho bullshit where you are trying to protect us. If one of them tries to hurt you, you'll need someone there to make sure you come back to me."

"Okay," he says softly as he pulls me into a hug. "I'll always come back to you, Butterfly."

Eight chairs.

Eight rapists.

Eight plans for revenge.

I am sitting on the metal table next to Allison as Nash and Daniel ensure that all the men are secured to their chairs. They are not awake yet. They likely have concussions, but that's the least of their worries right now.

Stan Fields, Carl Richards, Colton Barlow, Edgar Sanchez, Jerome Williams, Ivan Sinclair, Brad Harrington, Tony Marchetti. They don't look like monsters when they are unconscious. A month ago, they nearly destroyed my life. It shattered my life to pieces, but Nash took those pieces and made me who I am today. I am not just Lila. I am Wraith's Butterfly. It's time I spread my wings and fly into their nightmares. I will become the monster they failed to be for me.

"So, how do you want this done?" Nash asks me.

"Colton, Carl, Ivan, Tony, and Brad... can we decapitate them?" I ask and Nash smiles.

"We sure can," he says.

"So, now that we've seen the pictures from your assault when you went to the hospital... Can I help?" Allison asks.

"Oh, of course," I say. "Wanna roll some heads?"

"That sounds bloody amazing," she says and we both giggle.

One after another, they start to wake up. They look disoriented, but they understand what's going on when they pull at their restraints. Nash goes to the storage closet and gets out three more bone saws, then hands one to Daniel, Allison, and me.

"W-What are you doing?" Colton asks, wide eyed. I ignore him and look at Nash.

"I'll take Colton, since he spoke first," I say.

"I'll take Carl and Ivan then," Nash says. I nod and move to stand behind Colton.

I grab Colton by the hair, and he instantly falls hysterical as I bring the serrated blade to his throat. I know he is begging, but I am entirely focused on how it feels to hold a knife to someone. I let all of the emotions from that night come to the surface, but this time, I am in control with how they affect me. I get to choose how I react.

I press in deep as I slowly rip into his throat. I take my time sawing through his flesh as blood is gushing from his neck and spilling down his chest. His gurgled screams are intoxicating. The human body holds about ten pints of blood, and I am watching it all rush to exit through the gash in his neck that I am still sawing into. His blood pressure is up, so it's spraying from his body and coating everything in his vicinity. The other men are screaming at us to stop, but we don't. We are all lost in this bloodlust that they created when they attacked me.

I keep cutting, even after his body goes limp. I apply just enough pressure to feel tendons pop and snap free. I hit the spine and work my way through the bone before his head detaches from his body entirely. After I drop the knife, I turn his head so that I can see his face.

"He looks better this way," I say as I stare into the frightened eyes of my rapist. The look that his death leaves on his face reminds me of how I felt during and after the rape. I felt separate from my body as the weight of my trauma crushed me. I didn't want to heal because healing meant I had to face what they had done. I am facing it now and moving on looks glorious from this point of view.

I set Colton's head in his lap before turning to the others. They have all done the same with their bodies. When I look at Stan, Jerome, and Edgar, they are deathly pale.

"You are fucking insane," Stan says with a shaky voice that he is trying to hide.

"Just wait," I smile. "I'm saving you for last."

Nash, Daniel, and Allison move over to the table while I move to stand in front of Edgar. He is sobbing. Snot is coming out of his nose as tears stream down his cheeks. He understands his fate, but he has no idea what I'm about to do. I'm sure he is anticipating the same death that his friends received, but I have different plans for him.

"You were the second one to rape me," I say.

"I'm sorry," he sobs. "Please, I'm sorry."

"Save it," I say with a smirk. "We both know you are just trying to save your life. You were not sorry when you pissed on me, were you?"

"I'm sorry," he says with a broken voice. I thought it would take more to break the man who was the first to step forward when Stan gave them free run of me, but I'm not disappointed.

"What do you need?" Nash asks.

"Water, a cloth, and for someone to lay his chair back.

"Oh, that's easy," Allison says as she moves closer. I burst out laughing when she kicks him in the chest and his chair tips back. He makes a grunting sound before he cries out from the fall.

Nash brings over the items I requested and kisses me gently, pulling my attention away from my rapists. "Don't get lost in this feeling the way I did," he says with a soft tone. "Getting justice for yourself will feel better than anything you have ever experienced, but you can't get lost in it."

"Okay," I say with a smile. He kisses me once more before going back to stand with Daniel and Allison. The other two men are dead silent but watching my every move as I lay the cloth over Edgar's face.

When I pick up the water, I let myself think about what he did to me. The evil I saw in his eyes as he stared down at me still haunts my nightmares. These three men took the most from me, so I will take everything from them. He carelessly slapped me over and over until I submitted to him and his abuse. He forcefully fucked me while I bled. He didn't care that I begged him not to do it. He didn't care that I was sobbing and shaking. It wasn't about the sex for him. He craved the power that he had over me in that moment.

I start pouring the ice-cold water on his face. A stream splashes over his nose and mouth as he thrashes his head back and forth to try to get the sensation of drowning to stop. He gurgles and coughs as the water starts to choke him. I don't let up. I keep pouring and Nash hands me another jug of water to continue. He is trying to breathe, but he can't get the buildup of water out of his airway. The water quickly fills his nasal cavity and throat. His body convulses as he pulls on his restraints, but I keep pouring. His movements weaken and his body jerks a few more times before his body stills and becomes lifeless.

A sudden wave of mental anguish slams down on me and I drop the jug and back away. Nash and Daniel get to me and stop me from moving. Nash holds my face in his hands but I feel suddenly detached from reality. Daniel has his hands on my waist to keep me still and I match my breathing to theirs.

"Talk to me," Nash says quietly.

"I… I hate that I loved that," I reply. "I feel as evil as them."

"You are not evil, Butterfly," he says sweetly. "Evil people hurt good people. As a society, it should be normalized to give back the abuse that the scum of the Earth forces onto undeserving souls. You were an innocent woman walking down the street when they attacked you. You did not deserve for your boyfriend to pay scum to kill you for money. You never should have been groomed by that bastard. You should've been protected. No one seemed to give a shit that you were innocent and undeserving of the pain. You are taking control over your life, and I see nothing wrong with that."

"Why does doing that make me… What is wrong with me that watching someone die turns me on?" I ask.

"If you figure it out, let me know," Nash chuckles.

"Watching you get lost in the process is a kink I never knew I had," Daniel says before kissing my neck. I relax with a sigh, and both men chuckle.

"Watch it, Lila. I have no problem fucking you in front of the men you're about to murder," Nash says with a devious grin.

"Mmm. Prove it," I say, matching his smile. He looks behind at Daniel and nods. Daniel then turns me to face him before he grabs the back of my thighs and picks me up. My dress rides up as I wrap my legs around him and he carries me to the metal table. Allison moves to the two remaining men and slaps tape over their mouths before she finds scissors to cut their clothes off.

"What are you doing?" Nash asks with a laugh.

"I want to see how much they like watching her get fucked." She shrugs. "Can I fuck with them?"

"Fuck with them or assault them?" Daniel asks with a laugh.

"I'll edge them or make them repeatedly come. I haven't decided yet," she says.

"Definitely repeated orgasms. It's only appropriate considering they forced one on me," I say.

"I got you," she says with a smile.

"If you want to make it fun, grab the syringe in the cabinet that is labeled Trimix," Nash says. "There are other items you could use."

"You are a freak and I love it," Allison says with a laugh as she looks in the cabinet.

Daniel and Nash turn their attention to me to get me out of my underwear. Having their hands on me sent me to a peaceful place in my mind. Daniel lays back with his feet still on the floor before I shift to pull his cock free. "Jesus, I forgot how big you are," I groan.

"Oh, they're going to wreck you," Allison says with a giggle. I glance back at her, and she is injecting something into Jerome's dick. Before I can comment, Daniel pulls me down and surges his cock into my pussy. "Oh fuck!"

"Jesus, you're tight," Daniel growls. I place my hands on his chest and bounce on his cock as he lifts his hips to push deeper. Nash grabs me by the hair and jerks my head back to roughly kiss me. When my movements begin to falter, Daniel tightens his grip and starts fucking me hard and fast from below.

"Fuck. Oh fuck," I moan.

"Look at you, Lila," Nash says sweetly. "My slutty little Butterfly. Do you like the way he fucks you, baby?"

"Yes," I whimper. "I need more. I need you."

"So eager," Nash chuckles. He moves away from me for a few seconds and returns to stand behind me just as I hear the cap of a bottle open. Daniel pulls me down to his chest and stops while he is buried to the hilt inside of me. When Nash slowly fills my ass with his cock, I stiffen. Daniel takes my face in his hands to force me to look at him.

"Relax, Lila," he says softly. "We want to make you feel good."

"Please don't hurt me," I whisper. Despite my hesitance, my body relaxes and allows Nash to push deeper.

"We've got you, Butterfly," Nash groans as he fills me completely. "We will be gentle."

"No. I don't want gentle," I say hurriedly.

"What do you want, sweetie. Talk to us," Nash says.

"Just make it feel good. I need more," I say as my body tightens around their cocks.

Daniel wraps his arms around my body to pin me against his chest while Nash holds me by the waist. When they start to move, they instantly fall into a pace together that makes me scream out as they start to pound into my body. The muffled screaming from the men fuel something in all of us as we are tangled together in the basement of a funeral home.

"Oh, Butterfly. So greedy. Always wanting more," Nash rumbles as he grabs me by the hair and pulls me up to my knees. Daniel moves his hands to my hips as they alternate their thrusts.

"Oh, God. I'm gonna come," I whimper as they aggressively fuck me. Nash wraps his arms around me to cup my breast and pinches at my nipple. I let out a gasp as I feel his warm breath on my skin followed by the sharp pain of his teeth biting down into the soft flesh where my neck meets my shoulder. He wraps his other hand around my throat and squeezes.

"That's my good girl, Butterfly. Take it all," he growls in my ear. The pressure in my belly reaches its peak and an explosive orgasm rips though me. My body goes rigid as I come, and I can't draw a breath in. It feels as though it's trapped inside of me. When he loosens his grip, I gasp for breath and I am sucked into a catatonic state as they fall into their orgasm together.

Nash picks me up and cradles me in his arms before I can collapse. I am so dazed that all I can manage to do is snuggle into his chest more as he carries me off somewhere. Before he can lay me anywhere, I fall asleep.

Chapter Eighteen

Nash

I LAY LILA ON the couch in my office, clean her up, and fix her clothing before covering her with a blanket. I sit beside her and move her head into my lap as Daniel and Allison come in.

"Hey. She good?" Daniel asks.

"Yeah. She just crashed from the adrenaline," I say as I gently stroke her hair. "They secure down there?"

"Yeah. They are not very happy about being left with dead bodies, but they are secure," Allison says. "It was way more fun torturing them than I thought."

"You had entirely too much fun," Daniel laughs. "I didn't know you could bruise a dick with a pump."

"We learn something new every day," she shrugs.

"How are you two handling this?" I ask.

"You mean cutting someone's head off?" Daniel asks and I nod. "Honestly, man... there is something rewarding about helping her get justice for what they did to her. Those pictures of her bruises and just her overall appearance at the hospital... they deserved far worse than what she gave them."

"I agree," I say. "But... she picked what she did because it was important to her. I can't imagine how she felt going through what they did."

"Yeah," Daniel sighs. "When I met her and Mildred right after... I don't think I have ever seen someone so broken."

"What was she like before the rape?" Allison asks.

"I only really interacted with her at work, but she was always smiling and upbeat. No matter what was going on, she was happy. I've noticed that she is starting to let some of that back in, but she doesn't see the world in the same way she used to. Not everything is sunshine and roses anymore, so I think there are some pieces of her that will never return."

"I don't think that's a bad thing," I say. "But I also think that before it wasn't that she didn't know that evil existed, she was just responding to that trauma in her life differently than she did with the attack."

"I agree," Daniel states. "I do think she is past the worst of it though. Once she accepted that she wanted to live, she's been more receptive to us helping her out of those dark places she goes to sometimes."

"She is pretty good at coming to me when she gets overwhelmed. I've been working from home a lot, so she has slowly been venturing back into her work as well."

"Yeah, I saw that she's been working on one of the smaller projects," Daniel says. "She is insanely smart."

"She is," I agree. "I am curious what she will do with the other two."

"Let's hope it hurts," Allison says.

Chapter Nineteen

Lila

I SLEPT FOR A few hours in Nash's office before I finally woke up. I don't know why I was so tired, but I must have needed it. Now I am watching as Nash and Daniel move the dead bodies while Stan and Jerome sit tied to their chairs, face to face.

Nash and Daniel join Allison at the metal table where I have everything laid out. Both men are fighting back tears, and it's glorious to see them so broken, is like a dream come true.

"Jerome," I say, and he flinches. "You're up, since I'm saving Stan for last." He is mumbling something, so I go over and rip the tape off his mouth.

"Why are you doing this?" he asks. "Please don't do this."

"You smeared dog shit on me, Jerome," I say. "You raped me anally and added to my injuries."

I go over to the table and put on a pair of latex gloves before grabbing the tape and the bag of fresh dog shit that Allison got for me after running back to their house to check on their mastiff named Bruno. Allison grabs gloves and walks over with me. "Just hold his mouth open so he doesn't bite me," I say.

"Open wide, Jerome," I say as Allison forces his mouth open. He starts shaking his head and trying to pull away from her while I get the shit out of the bag with a gloved hand. The pungent smell and still-warm slimy texture nearly makes me gag, so I quickly shove it into his mouth before Allison forces it shut so I can apply the tape.

Jerome immediately starts retching and his eyes go wide. He is pulling hard on his restraints while he desperately tries to not puke. It only takes a few seconds for him to lose his fight and he gags as his throat and body spasm. He starts to violently shake as the forceful expulsion of puke and dog feces flood from his nose. It's not coming out fast enough though. He begins to choke on shitty vomit, as he is forced to continuously aspirate causing him to make a muffled glorious gurgling sound as he slowly drowns.

He continues to spew out of his nose, and he has pure terror painted on his face. After a few minutes, his body goes limp. He has a rancid mixture of puke and fecal matter all over his face and chest. His eyes are bulging from straining so hard. You can still see the fear in his eyes, even after the life within has dwindled away.

"Damn," Nash says. "I loved that more than I thought I would."

"Oh... But I have something even better planned for Stan," I say deviously, and he chuckles as he turns to help prepare the Piranha solution. I go to Stan and Daniel helps me force a tube into his mouth before we tape it into place. It is about three inches wide, so the acid will be able to flow quickly down his throat.

"What is he mixing?" Daniel asks me.

"That... is sulphuric acid and hydrogen peroxide," I say. "Piranha solution vaporizes everything made of carbon."

"Which is everything," he laughs.

"Exactly. It ate though the motel manager's chest in short order. I can't wait to see what it does from the inside out."

Stan starts to scream something at me, but I don't understand what he is saying, nor do I care. I smirk at him and eventually he gives up.

"I made you a quart. That should be more than enough to do the job and not make cleanup too terrible," Nash says. "Want me to pour?"

"No, I've got it. I just don't want to get splashed if he coughs up blood," I say humorously.

"When he coughs it up," he corrects me. "Put on gear. All of you." We all put on protective gear, and I move over to stand in front of Stan.

"You understand why I am doing this, right?" I ask. He nods and he looks absolutely broken. "I wanted you to watch as all your friends... the ones you sent after me... die slowly and painfully. I want you to feel everything they felt and everything I felt... You hurt me, humiliated me, degraded me, and broke me. You destroyed my life because my idiot ex-boyfriend wanted money. You failed to do your job correctly, but I won't. I'm going to sit here and watch the light leave your eyes. After, we will put your body in that incinerator. You will burn to ash, and I will flush you down the toilet. No one will miss you. No one will look for you. You will just be an awful nightmare that everyone forgets about... Ready?"

He is sobbing hysterically as he faces his inevitable death. He doesn't nod but he doesn't object. He knows it doesn't matter. He didn't give me a choice, so I'm sure as fuck not going to give him a choice.

Nash lifts me to stand on a chair beside Stan so I can pour the mixture into the funnel that is angled to send it directly down his throat. When the beaker is handed off to me, he squeezes his eyes shut. He is shaking so hard that he is convulsing. I glance up at Nash and I am giddy with excitement.

"Bottoms up," I say as I dump the clear liquid down the tube. He screams and it takes him a few seconds to realize that it's just water. He coughs and chokes a bit, but ultimately recovers.

"Now you know just how terrified I was when you grabbed me," I say. "Now you know what it's like to face death and not be able to do a damn thing about it because someone else made a choice for you."

"Good?" Nash asks me as Daniel walks up from behind to hand me the beaker of solution.

"Yes," I say happily, and Stan relaxes. What a fool. Doesn't he know he destroyed who I once was? The blood and bruises were like a knife to my soul, but the humiliation is what twisted that blade and broke me. I will never be whole again. I will always remember what it was like to be attacked by evil. I will be able to recall the evil in his eyes as he made me vomit. His laughter will play on a loop in the back of my head until the day I die. I will never escape what he did to me, so he will never escape what I'll do to him.

Stan is no longer shaking; he feels safe. I grip onto the beaker, and I still have the funnel in my other hand. I quickly dump the solution into the funnel. Daniel grabs me from the chair to pull me away when his pained screams gurgle up the tube and a mixture of blood and acid spray out a little.

I move to stand with Nash, he is standing behind me with his arms around me. Daniel is next to him and holds Allison similarly. We watch the carnage unfold and I can't help but laugh at his screams.

Stan's screams are reduced to just groans. It doesn't take long for the solution to dissolve through his vital organs and his body goes limp. The skin in his throat, mouth, and chest are turning a putrid green and black color as the solution burns though his body.

I stand and stare at his now dead body as tears silently roll down my cheeks. I have no regrets and I'm glad they are dead, but it still hurts. I never expected the pain to dissipate entirely but, in this moment, it hurts just the same as it did before. Having Nash hold me while I cry is the solace that I needed all along. Life seems manageable now, even with all the pain.

Nash and Daniel load the bodies on carts, and they are taken up stairs. We get them situated in the ovens. There are four, so we put two in each. It will take longer but not as long as doing them individually.

I resume sleeping in Nash's lap while Allison does the same with Daniel. The guys keep an eye on the cameras to ensure no one shows up. Lucky for us, tomorrow is Saturday, and no one has to get up early.

I think it's time that I went back to work. I have done some work here and there from home, but I'm starting to get restless being inside all day. I'm starting to feel like myself again, only a different version of who I used to be.

Once the bodies are incinerated, we let the oven cool then sweep out ash. We put it all into one container before taking it to the bathroom. Little by little, we flush the remains and erase them from the Earth. They cannot hurt anyone else; they cannot hurt me.

I feel confident moving forward in the world. The more time goes by, the more I feel like I'm wasting my life away feeling sorry for myself in the house. I want to do more than survive now. I want to live.

Chapter Twenty

Nash

Three Months Later

THE LAST THREE MONTHS with Lila have been like a dream come true. Before her, I always had the urge to hunt and make someone bleed for their darkness. I still see the darkness in people, but I no longer crave hearing their screams. I simply pray to whatever divine being is out there that they will erase them from the world.

Lila has been getting better as well. After killing her rapists, she went into a depressed state for a few days, but she never stopped fighting. She didn't let herself sink as far as she did after the attack. The sudden adrenaline took a lot out of her, but she still got up every day. It took about a week, but she returned to the office, and she has been thriving.

Daniel and I decided to move her office closer to mine. I am a bit leery about Jeff still being out there and angry at her. Jessika disappeared from his life and got an abortion when she found out what Jeff did. They talk, but Lila is cautious with her. She understands that what he did to her wasn't consensual, but it still hurt that it happened. Jessika is understanding and is being very patient with Lila. Although she doesn't have any other choice but to be patient, she isn't giving up.

We know that Jeff is watching Lila. Although I know I could keep her locked away where he can't get to her, we know what is going to have to happen. I just hope that Lila can handle it when the time comes.

I am standing in the doorway of the kitchen, watching Lila cook dinner. She's wearing a long, loose dress. It will be convenient so I can hike it up and fuck her to tears. We have an unspoken agreement of free use, and I think now is a perfect time to remind her again who she belongs to.

She has not noticed me, so I quietly walk up behind her and put my hands on either side of the counter, blocking her. "Run, Butterfly," I whisper in her ear. "Run or you will be mine to use."

"Oh shit," Lila giggles. She pushes away from me and bolts out of the kitchen. Before she can get too far, I grab her by the hair and pull her back against my chest.

"No safe word. No way out. If I catch you... I'll make it hurt," I say with a threatening tone. She swallows hard and nods, likely speechless. "Go on my sweet prey. Let me hunt you."

When I release her, she runs. We both know I could catch her in short order, but I'll let her have her fun for a while. I pull the pot off the stove and saunter after her. No one is supposed to be here for another hour, so we have time to play.

She giggles when she hears my footsteps that I make no effort to quiet. She is awful at hide and seek, but we all know that she wants to be found. She thrives the most when she gives complete control over to me. Although we play it like she has no choice, she does. I know exactly when to stop and she knows that I will. She and I thoroughly enjoy her playing the role of the innocent victim while I play the psychotic attacker who loves to make her scream. It's not a lie though. I do love to make her scream. I haven't done anything too intense yet, but today is the day I think it's important to remind her that she is in control.

I step into the living room at the same time as she does from the hallway. She is trying to find a place to hide, but I've already locked the doors, so she has nowhere to go. I am forcing her to take the stairs and she knows exactly why.

Lila makes a beeline for the staircase, and I let her get about halfway up before I grab her ankle. "You thought you could escape me, Butterfly?" I ask as I pull her arms behind her back and pin them with one hand while pulling her dress up with the other.

"Let go of me," she demands, playing along as she wiggles under my grip on her. I ignore her and yank her panties off. Before I go any further, I pull the ping-pong ball from my pocket and put it in her hand. This is my way of telling her that she's not going to be able to call her safe word. She grips tightly to the small white ball in her hand, and I pull my cock free. I am painfully hard, and I can't get into her quick enough. "Wait. No. Don't," she yells at me. She sounds so believable, which just makes me want to fuck her harder.

Ignoring her again, I cover her mouth and surge into her dripping cunt. I groan when I bottom out and she screams against my hand. I offer no reprieve as I start to fuck her hard and fast. I let go of her hands so I can hike her leg up and push deeper. She is moaning and whimpering but I can feel her tears rolling down her face and across the back of my hand. She is gripping me like a fucking vice, and it makes me moan as I continue my near violent thrusting. When I readjust my hold on her she grabs the banister and attempts to pull herself away. I move my hand that is covering her mouth to the side of her face as I pin her cheek against the stairs.

"I'm going to fuck this tight little cunt and you're going to lay here and take it like the filthy whore you are," I growl in her ear and thrust hard to put emphasis on my words. She cries out with each stroke, but she still has a tight hold on that ball.

"Please. Stop," she cries. I laugh when she tightens her muscles around my cock, practically begging me for more.

"Scream, Lila. Beg me to stop," I say loudly.

"*Please*!" she yells. "*Please stop*!"

"Come for me, bitch. Come on my cock."

"I don't want to," she lies. "Please don't make me come... Please... I don't want to come."

I pull out for just long enough so I can flip her to her back and slam back into her. She arches her back and moans loudly but grabs the banister to continue to try to pull herself out from under me. She doesn't try hard, but she ends up moving her hands to my chest to try and push me away.

"Fight me, whore. Try harder," I growl at her. She is quickly slipping out of character as she closes in on her orgasm. I wrap my hand around her throat and squeeze before pinching her clit hard. Her body shudders violently but she is completely silent as she is unable to take a breath. I gently kiss her lips when they turn a beautiful shade of blue. Just as her eyes roll back and they are about to flutter closed, I release my grip and she sucks in a big breath of oxygen. She immediately falls into her orgasm. She practically throws the ball before wrapping her arms around my neck and pulling me against her body.

"Oh God. Yes," she moans loudly as she clings to me. "Please. Harder. Oh God, Nash. Please, come in me."

Our moans are desperate as our tongues greedily explore one another through our kiss as our orgasms synchronize. When I come, I push deep before draining myself inside the love of my life.

"Fuck, I love you," Lila pants as I pull out of her.

"I love you too, Butterfly," I say sweetly before gently kissing her. "Let's get cleaned up before everyone gets here."

I set the salad on the table before taking my seat beside Lila. Jessika is on her other side. Daniel and Allison are across from us, and Mildred is at the head of the table.

"How was everyone's day?" Jessika asks.

"Rough," Lila says with a giggle.

"Are you okay? What's wrong?" Jessika asks worriedly. It clicks when Lila laughs and Jessika laughs with her.

"You two have more sex than anyone I've ever met," Daniel says.

"If you can't compete, it's okay to admit it. Sometimes with age, men can struggle to get an erection," Lila says with a sweet smile.

"Brat," Daniel says, narrowing his eyes.

"Old man," she retorts with a giggle.

"Little girl, I will bend you over this table," he threatens.

"And what? Flaccid hump me until you throw out your back?" she asks and Daniel growls.

"You did throw out your back that one time we fucked on the floor," Allison laughs.

"Okay, children," Mildred laughs. "Eat. Lila and Jessika have plans."

"Oh, that's right!" Allison says happily. "What are you two planning?"

"Dancing and drinking like the old days before she moved in," I say with a smile. "We won't be out too late."

"Be careful, Lila," Daniel says seriously.

"I will. I promise," she says softly.

"Let's eat," I say. "It's going to be a fun night."

Chapter Twenty-One

Lila

I RINSE MY PLATE and put it in the dishwasher before I go upstairs to get ready. I haven't been out since the night I was attacked four months ago. It feels weird to be getting ready to go out without Nash, but I'm glad Jessika agreed to come with me. We have done a lot of work over the last few months, and I think this is what we both need to move forward.

Once I am dressed and everything is in place, I go downstairs to meet the others. I am wearing a knee-length, black bodycon style dress with long sleeves. I have it paired with black knee-high boots and my hair is falling down my back in beautiful blonde curls.

"You look stunning," Nash says when he turns to look at me.

"Thanks," I say with a smile as I kiss him. "I'll text you when we leave."

"Please do, and stay together," he says.

"Yes, Dad," Jessika laughs as she hooks her arm in mine. "We will be okay."

"What she said," I laugh.

"Not gonna ditch her this time?" Daniel asks bitterly.

"Nah. I figured I'd save that for when she least expects it," Jessika says with a wink.

"You're more of a brat than she is," Daniel says, shaking his head. Daniel tries to hide how he feels but he is also trying to come around to trusting her. The only interaction he has had with her until now is tied to my trauma.

"Oh, lighten up," Allison laughs. "We will see you two later. Be safe."

"We will," I say as Daniel hugs me.

"I don't like this," he says softly so only I can hear him.

"I know," I reply. "I'll be okay."

Daniel holds onto me for a second, rubbing my back, before kissing my temple. "Go on. Have fun," he says, releasing me.

I kiss Nash one last time before Jessika and I go to my car. We drive to the office and park in my reserved spot before stepping out onto the sidewalk and walk toward the club. We are going to the same one we went to the night of my rape. Jessika is stuck to me like glue, and I can tell she's nervous. She's never been good at hiding her emotions.

Jessika and Nash have helped me a lot with my binging and purging problems. For whatever reason, it is my go-to when I am stressed, but it didn't start until those men raped me. I was hoping it would go away when they died, but it didn't. It got bad enough that I had Nash be completely in charge of what I ate and when I would finish, he would sit and hold me for a while so I couldn't go make myself throw up. Maybe that's controlling in a way, but I have no self-control apparently.

Little by little, he started giving me more control over what I ate and how much. Now, I have the wherewithal to slow down and ask for help when I need it. Daniel and Allison are supportive of my struggles. They know if I come to them, I'm looking for someone to take control of me for a moment because I know I am unable to have a reasonable amount of self-control. Last week, I was stressed about a project, and I spiraled on my lunch break. I went to Daniel, and I didn't even have to say it before he shut and locked his office before holding me in his lap for most of my lunch break. He called Nash down when he got out of his meeting and together, they pulled me out of that dark place in my mind.

When we get to the club, we get a drink before going to the dance floor. We stay together and enjoy the music. It feels nice to have my friend by my side again. Jeff nearly ruined the both of us.

We hang out for a few hours before getting some water and stepping out onto the sidewalk. We link arms and walk toward the car.

"Is it weird walking this way?" Jessika asks.

"Uh. Not really," I say. "It probably should be."

"Where is the flower shop?"

"We are coming up on it," I say. I hear footsteps behind us and when I glance back, I see that it's Jeff. "Jeff is following us."

"Just keep walking," Jessika says. I nod and we continue to walk toward the car. As we get to the flower shop, a hand grabs my arm and Jessika moves away from me. I knew it was going to happen, but I still gasp and try to pull my arm away. He pushes me against the old building and puts his hands on the brick, trapping me.

"Good to see you, darling," he says with a snarky tone.

"What do you want?" I ask flatly.

"You," he growls. "You left me."

"You fucked my best friend then tried to have me killed for money. Duh," I say. "What the fuck did you expect? Never mind the fact that you repeatedly fucked and injured me when I was fourteen, while making me believe it was love."

"Your new little boyfriend not teach you any manners?" he asks.

"No, he just fucks me well enough that I am well behaved," I say with a smile. He rears back and slaps me across the face, and I laugh.

"Is that it?" I ask, still chuckling.

"You know, I was just going to shoot you in the head and get this over with, but I think I'll have a little fun first," he says as he grabs me by the hair and drags me into the flower shop. "Shut the door, Jessika."

"You're helping him?" I yell at her.

"I love him," she says. "I never should have aborted our baby."

"You fucking bitch," I shout. Jeff shoves me down to a familiar mattress and panic suddenly rises as the smell of this dilapidated building makes my brain flood with memories. I try to stop myself but once I acknowledge the panic, it consumes me.

"That's it, bitch. Fight me," Jeff laughs as I slap at him and try to push him off me as he forces my legs apart.

"Stop it, Jeff," I yell. I'm trying to not lose complete control, but when he covers my mouth, I start crying.

"Don't worry, Lila, I'll make sure Nash knows I was the last one inside your used up pussy," he says as he pulls my arms up above my head to pin them as he rips my underwear off and readies himself to thrust into me.

"Don't. You don't want to do this," I warn.

"Oh, but I do," he says seriously. "You will always belong to me, Lila. Always."

Jeff buries himself balls deep but screams out in pain almost immediately. When he pulls away from me, he takes the anti-rape condom with him.

I saw an article about a female condom with spikes to help prevent rape in South Africa. Rape-axe was invented by Sonette Ehlers after having met multiple rape victims. It basically allows the man's penis to enter, but the teeth-like barbs keep the device attached and will rip into the flesh of the man who tried to rape someone.

Jeff is jerked away from me, and Nash pulls me up and fixes my clothes before hugging me tightly. Jessika joins the hug as I start nearly sobbing.

"It's okay. We've got you," Nash says softly.

"I'm sorry," Jessika says tearfully.

"It's okay," I say as I hug her back. "Thank you for your help."

"We both deserve this," she says. "Let's get rid of this fucker."

I step back and wipe my tears away before turning to see that Daniel has Jeff sitting on the ground with his hands behind his back, tied around a support beam.

Jeff looks raging mad but doesn't say a word. I can see on his face that he is in pain. "Not very talkative now, are we?" I ask as I bring myself down to my knees beside him.

"I think he wants that thing off of him," Jessika says as she kneels on his other side.

"It's going to be hard but… I think we should help him," I say with a devious smile.

"Don't you fucking…" his words are cut off when I wrap my hand around his dick. His breathing is coming in short bursts, and he squeezes his eyes shut.

"Never seen a man so terrified to get his dick touched before," Allison cackles. "Twist it, then yank it off."

"Good idea," I say.

"Lila. Please. Please don't," Jeff chokes out.

"You know… Jerome begged me too," I say. "Wanna know how that ended for him?"

"How?" Jeff asks in a quiet voice.

"I shoved dog shit in his mouth before sealing it shut with tape," I say, and his eyes go wide. "He drowned on his puke and Daniel's dog's shit... Stan... Stan died when I poured acid down his throat... Edgar was waterboarded to death. The others were decapitated."

"Why are you doing this?" Jeff asks tearfully. "What does this solve?"

"This isn't about solving anything, Jeff," I say firmly. "This is about making you pay for what you did to me for all those years... for using me and breaking me. This is for trying to have me killed but getting me raped by eight men at once. This is for you, raping my best friend into submission and isolating the both of us. I nearly killed myself because of you. Hell, I *tried* to kill myself because of you."

"I'm sorry," he says weakly. "Please don't do this."

"It's too late for apologies," I say as I twist the barbed condom, making him let out a blood-curdling scream. Jessika and I laugh before I yank it off. The barbs of the Rape-axe have ripped into his flesh and he is bleeding from the jagged gashes left behind. He continues to scream until I get sick of it and grab my underwear from the floor that he tore off my body. I shove it into his mouth, then Jessika takes tape from Daniel to shut Jeff up.

"What now?" Jessika asks.

"Now we have some fun," I laugh. "Can you guys get him across the chair?" I gesture to the dirty chair in the corner and Nash laughs.

They move him so that he is lying across the seat and his arms are secured to the legs. I pull his pants down the rest of the way, and he is sobbing. He knows what I'm going to do.

"Pick an item, Nash," I say.

"Easy," Nash says. "Broom handle." He hands me a disgusting broom from the floor that looks as though it's been sitting here for a decade.

"Perfect," I say. I look at Jessika and she gives me her nod of approval, so I line up the tip of the broomstick with his ass as I shove it into him without warning. He screams behind the tape as I fuck him in the ass with the splintered wooden handle. I force it as deep as I can, trying to cause as much damage as possible. When there is resistance, I push until it pops and ruptures, blood mixed with stool starts pouring out of his ass. Everyone laughs when we realize that I have caused intestinal damage.

His screams turn to whimpers and his whimpers turn into weakened groans until he eventually goes limp. I take the handle out, it's covered in blood. I toss it to the ground and turn to Nash and the others. "Someone finish this. I'm done," I say coldly. Jessika takes a switch blade from Daniel and grabs Jeff by the hair to pull his head back.

"Good riddance," she mumbles before dragging the blade across his neck. Blood sprays out as she hits major arteries. When he drops his head, she drops the knife then stands up and hugs me.

"It's done," I say. "Thank you."

"Anything for you," she says softly. "I'm sorry I didn't protect you more. I thought by letting him do what he was doing that you'd be safe."

"It's okay," I say. "I forgive you. Just... don't touch Nash."

"He scares me," she laughs.

"And Daniel doesn't?" Nash asks with a laugh.

"No. He's like a gummy bear," she shrugs.

"That's funny, considering the whole erectile dysfunction thing," I say. I yell when Daniel grabs me by the hair and yanks me to him. He wraps his hand around my throat and brings me nose to nose with him.

"You're pushing it, little girl," he warns.

"You have to be careful with me now," I say with a grin, and he immediately matches my smile.

"Oh, I'll be careful when I fuck that sassy little mouth of yours," he says.

"Are you two talking in code?" Nash asks and Daniel nods in his direction.

"Go on. Tell your man," he says. I nod happily and move to stand in front of Nash. I loop my arms around his neck, and he grabs the backs of my thighs so he can pick me up. I wrap my legs around his waist and kiss him.

"What's up?" he asks.

"I'm pregnant," I say, trying to contain my happiness.

"Oh my God!" he says with a large smile. "I thought..."

"I know you want kids and I want kids, so I had the birth control removed so I could surprise you. I'm five weeks."

"Well... then you should know that what I had planned for our date night tomorrow was planned before I knew this," he says. It takes me a second to get it but when I do, I gasp loudly.

"Wait really?" I ask.

"Mhmm," he smiles. "The ring is at home."

"Yes!"

"Do you want to see the ring?" he laughs.

"I don't care what it looks like! Yes!" I say as I kiss him hard then lay my head on his shoulder.

"Take her home," Daniel says. "We can handle him."

"You sure?" Nash asks.

"I am. Go on," he says.

"Take me home and play with me," I say with a conniving grin.

"Oh, how can I resist your offer, my sweet Butterfly," Nash says, kissing me with a grin as we leave Jeff and the past behind.

About the author

Emily Klepp is a Western North Carolina native residing in eastern Tennessee with her loving husband and two beautiful children. She has been writing since she was fourteen years old as a way to cope with her anxiety. She hopes to help others be able to speak their truth by writing about topics that are considered too taboo for societal norms.

Books by this author

https://www.edknovels.com/books

How to contact the author

https://linktr.ee/emilykleppnovels

Printed in Dunstable, United Kingdom

65563420R00107